LOVE S

Pran Nevile was born and ....guished career in the Indian For... ....ce and the United Nations, he turned a freelance writer and has specialized in the study of the social and cultural history of India.

He has been invited by several distinguished institutions in India and also Universities in England and the U.S.A. to speak on themes related to Indian art and culture. He has also acted as consultant for two BBC films on the Raj.

He is the author of well known books such as *Lahore: A Sentimental Journey, Nautch Girls of India, Beyond the Veil, Rare Glimpses of the Raj, Stories from the Raj: Sahibs, Memsahibs and Others, K.L. Saigal: Immortal Singer* and his recent book: *Marvels of Indian Painting—Rise and Demise of Company School.*

He lives in Gurgaon.

ALSO BY PRAN NEVILE

Lahore: A Sentimental Journey
Nautch Girls Of The Raj

LOVE STORIES FROM
THE RAJ

Edited by

Pran Nevile

PENGUIN BOOKS

An imprint of Penguin Random House

PENGUIN BOOKS

USA | Canada | UK | Ireland | Australia
New Zealand | India | South Africa | China

Penguin Books is part of the Penguin Random House group of companies
whose addresses can be found at global.penguinrandomhouse.com

Published by Penguin Random House India Pvt. Ltd
7th Floor, Infinity Tower C, DLF Cyber City,
Gurgaon 122 002, Haryana, India

Penguin
Random House
India

First published by Penguin Books India 1995

ISBN 9780140252149

Typeset in Palatino by Digital Technologies and Printing Solutions, New Delhi
Printed at Repro India Limited

www.penguin.co.in

For
my grandchildren
Gaurika, Ravi, Aditya
Raman, Arjun and Anshuman

Contents

Foreword

Much has been written about the Raj by British and Indian authors, more perhaps than what the French, Dutch and the Portuguese have recorded about their connection with India. That India has been associated with all of them in varying degrees is, I regard, our good fortune. In our recorded history of five millennia we have a tapestry today in which are woven the cultures of Africa, Europe, and Central and West Asia. Two and a half millennia ago we traded with Africa, China, Central Asia, the legendary Spice Islands of South-East Asia, and Europe through Rome. And if we were invaded now and again throughout this period, we managed soon to integrate the conquerors and their culture. In fact, realization of this phenomenon caused the British to re-examine their position after 1857, and to make a conscious effort to pull away from this historic absorptive process of India. Aurangzeb too must have felt, consciously or unconsciously, that the Islamic-Mughal-Persian culture was being slowly absorbed by India. He deliberately reversed the process, and that was the beginning of the end of the Mughal Empire. It was India's strength and tradition that enabled the country to retain its basic cultural entity and beliefs intact.

After India became a part of the Queen's Empire, the

British in India also became aloof, living in their islands of cantonments and civil stations, sending their children home to school, looking down upon inter-marriage and its products. Everything local and native was shunned and disowned with an ill-concealed superiority. The Indian reaction was not unexpected, and from the new democratic culture of nineteenth century Europe, it created its own sense of nationalism. Half a century later, the British made an orderly departure; only a handful 'stayed on'. For the first time in our long history, the conquerors left as amicably as they had arrived, with their last consul presiding over the declaration of Indian independence at midnight.

Pran Nevile has done considerable research to dig out these tales, all left behind by the British, on the distaff side of their life—of men far away from home, living in loneliness in a culturally alien society where, deprived of home life, they found solace in the arms of local mistresses, whom their social mores prevented them from marrying. Problems inevitably arose, specially when, as the journey between home and India became shorter and more comfortable, their womenfolk began to arrive!

As a student of history, one can speculate on the if's of history: If the French had given Dupleix even half the support that Britain gave to Clive, and the Battle of Plassey had been won by the French, what would have been the shape of India, the Empire, indeed the world? And if the British had settled down in India completely like the Mughals and not remained aliens till the last, what would have been the texture of the Indian social and cultural life today?

It was in this context that Frank Anthony, the Anglo-Indian leader, in his book on the community, made his moving appeal to the departing British: 'Who are they O'

England but thy Sons!' The British took such care of the interests of the Muslims and Sikhs and other minorities as they left India but totally neglected their own sons.

In fact, Dennis Kincaid says that as the journey between Britain and India became shorter, and women began to come out to marry here, 'home' became no longer something to which only a few lived to return. With the development of fast steamboats and motor vessels reducing the journey between Bombay, Marseilles and Genoa to only eleven days, with a day more by the express trains to London, the British began to return home after two-and-a-half year spells to spend six months on leave. Their interest in India diminished until their service in India, with government, army or commerce, became an interlude between two home leaves. For months they talked about the next home leave and for months about the previous leave.

Apart from the love affairs of the departing 'sahibs', Pran Nevile has also written a book on their passion for performances by nautch girls. This will certainly be a useful addition to the series, particularly as this Mughal legacy to India has played an interesting role in the courts of kings and princes and the East India Company servants in the past centuries.

Prakash Tandon

Preface

Rich in historical and human interest, Raj literature comprising journals, diaries and memoirs provides a rare insight into British social life in India. Embedded in its numerous volumes are lively accounts of the private lives of sahibs and memsahibs interspersed with entertaining episodes and incidents. Modern writers in the recent spate of books on the Raj have tried to reconstruct this period of history from various aspects. They have, however, paid little attention to the love life of the white community to which this collection of stories is exclusively devoted. It grew out of my wanderings in a fascinating field of contemporary writings.

The love stories chiefly relate to the period from the middle of the eighteenth century, known as the 'Age of Nabobs', to the 'Age of Memsahibs' that dawned in the wake of the 1857 Mutiny. Selected with a view to recapturing the theme of love in all its glory and infamy, these are presented as they appeared in the original published texts, except that some of them have been given different titles and where required compressed for the sake of easy reading, and some spellings and punctuation have been modified, and obvious errors corrected, for similar reason. Background notes have been appended at the beginning of the stories.

The authors of these stories make it a point to emphasize

that they are faithful accounts of actual events. Even the characters are stated to be real personages though at times they bear changed names.

Like a good wine that needs no bush, a book if readable may not carry a preface. However, given the nature of this compilation, I have ventured to make a few preliminary observations. I hope the reader will not find them out of place.

Acknowledgements

In appreciation:
Members of the staff, India Office Library, London; India International Centre Library, New Delhi, who spared no pains to provide me with the reference material I needed.

Raj K. Kakar, Editorial Consultant, Sterling Publishers, New Delhi, who read the MS with me and made valuable suggestions for its improvement.

In gratitude:
Professor Robert L. Hardgrave Jr., University of Texas at Austin, USA; Professor Dennis Judd, North London University, London; Professor Ian Talbot, Coventry University, UK, who encouraged me in my research and assured me that the book was worth publishing.

And my friends Ashok Kumar, Baij Verma, and Prithvi Rishi in England and the USA for their gracious hospitality during my visits abroad in pursuit of my research.

Introduction

For the early British settlers in India life was a dreary existence. The heat and dust of the country, the tyranny of solitude and the dearth of means of recreation added to their miseries. Perhaps what they missed most was feminine company. The few European women who had accompanied their fortune-hunting husbands restricted their social intercourse to a small, select circle of friends. Access to the native gentry was almost impossible until a much later period when they came to learn, and even respect and admire, Indian manners and customs. With racial prejudice yet to make its ugly appearance, the men mixed freely with Indians on equal terms. Some eighteenth century sketches and drawings depict Englishmen, dressed in Indian clothing, lolling on cushions, smoking hookahs and enjoying nautch parties. The East India Company at one time tried to copy the Portuguese practice of playing the matchmaker by shipping batches of young women for its bachelor employees but the experiment failed. No wonder then that many a man fell into the arms of a native beauty.

The burgeoning Raj was thus very much a masculine affair. The women were honoured in their absence by the founders of the Empire who suffered prolonged separation from their wives and families. To rephrase a hoary catchphrase, the 'Empire was not acquired in a fit of absence of mind, so much as in a fit of absence of wives'. According to Ronald Hyam, a distinguished British historian, 'the enjoyment and exploitation of black flesh was as powerful an attraction as any desire to develop economic resources'. In the exotic realms of 'Hindostan', some of the European traders and adventurers found outlets for their surplus emotional and sexual energies which were somewhat suppressed in the more inhibited Britain.

Deterred by the perils of a long and tortuous voyage, few British women ventured to come to India until the late eighteenth century. Between 1700 and 1818 no less than 160 sailing ships of the East India Company were lost: burnt, seized or wrecked. Women from the captured ships were carried away by pirates and sold in the slave market at Surat from where some of them landed in the harems of Indian rulers.

The John Company employees who lacked moral or intellectual resources for a life of continence usually took Indian women as unofficial wives and mistresses. Until the end of the eighteenth century few of them could afford to maintain a European wife. The cost of landing one at Calcutta worked out at Rs. 5,000. Moreover, European wives expected to be provided with carriages, dressmakers, hairdressers, ladies' maids and nannies, which ordinary Company officials could ill afford. In these circumstances, keeping an Indian mistress provided not only a piece of sexual expediency, but also a very pleasant way of learning the language, customs and manners of the country and its people. They were like 'sleeping dictionaries'. Their 'upright, supple and slender, well-rounded limbs and their smooth skin of a bright chestnut colour' no doubt turned many a British male head. Liaisons were easy to arrange. Capt. Williamson in his famous guidebook *East India Vade Mecum* (1810) observed that the practice of keeping Indian mistresses was an economic necessity. 'It would be wrong,' he said, 'to conclude that these connections are made by choice to the neglect of our fair countrywomen.' There was nothing shameful or secret about these relationships and even the Governor of Bombay and members of his Council publicly admitted having native mistresses. The practice was also defended on the ground that it improved knowledge of local affairs, and some senior officers even encouraged it openly. Garnet Wolseley, who was in India just after the Mutiny, is said to have confessed to his brother that he consoled himself with a beautiful 'Eastern princess' who answered 'all the purposes of a wife without giving any of the bother; he had no wish to be caught in European marriage by 'some bitch', unless an heiress.

Samuel Brown, a Company official, recorded in his journal that 'the native women were so amusingly playful, so anxious to please, that a person after being accustomed to their society shrinks from the idea of encountering the whims, or yielding to the furies of an Englishwoman'. There was a Colonel who even agreed to be circumcised in order to get possession of a Muslim woman who imposed this condition before becoming his mistress.

For the greater part of the eighteenth century, the Company's servants were merchants who had come to India to make a fortune. A favourite after-dinner toast of those days was 'a lass and a lakh a day', a goal natural to men who saw a lakh of rupees a worthwhile object of ambition and a bibi, an Indian mistress, a fitting companion. Many Englishmen happily settled down with these women and raised families, but left them behind when returning to England. The pathos of such a parting is expressed in a ballad sung by an Indian bibi.

'Tis thy will and I must leave thee
of thou best beloved farewell
I forbear lest I should grieve thee,
Half my heart felt pangs to tell.
Soon a British fair will charm thee,
Thou alas her smiles must woo,
But tho' she to rapture warm thee
Don't forget thy poor Hindoo.

(*Anon*)

Children of these mixed unions, however, presented some problems. As they grew up they carried with them the stigma of illegitimacy. They were known as half-castes, Indo-Britons, East Indians and Eurasians until finally in the early twentieth century they were given the appellation 'Anglo-Indian', a nomenclature formerly applied to British men and women living in India. At different times Anglo-Indians occupied a different status on the Indian social scene. Until about 1785 they were accepted on an equal footing with the British. Senior Company officials sometimes sent their children for education to England. According to Anglo-Indian historians, three British Prime Ministers, the two Pitts and Lord Liverpool, are said to have had some Indian blood. From the beginning of the nineteenth century till 1835 Anglo-Indians were excluded from the East India Company's service. Later on however, they were provided jobs in certain services as Indians and in education and defence as British. They were mostly employed in railways, telegraphs and customs. The Indian caste system also affected the British attitude to

Anglo-Indians since the children of British fathers and native women were not accepted into their mothers' families.

From 1800 onwards, British women started arriving in India in increasing numbers to shop in its marriage bazaar. In that era of large families in England, for girls without dowry and charm, the only prospect was spinsterhood. Men who had amassed fortunes in India by fair means or foul— the so-called nabobs—were much sought after by parents and guardians of marriageable daughters. Even as early as the time of Clive, girls just out from home had been known as the newly arrived angels and there was keen competition to carry them ashore at Madras or to escort them from their carriages to the church at Calcutta.

As the nineteenth century rolled on and the frequency of sailings by the Company's Indiamen increased. The ships brought regular cargoes of venturesome beauties bent on matrimony. They grew into a social phenomenon known as the 'fishing fleet'. With this influx of women, Edinburgh came to be called the 'flesh market for the Indian marriage mart'. London sent supplies too. It was an age of quick marriages. Arrivals of young damsels, which were notified in the newspapers, were an exciting event for bachelors biding their time for a wife. On such occasions the captains of the ships and other well-known ladies of the settlement would organize grand parties where the candidates for wifehood 'sat up' for three or four nights in succession while the eligible bachelors, young and old, rushed there to try their luck. Matches were arranged on the spot while the ladies were on exhibition. The church on Sundays was also recognized as a marriage bazaar where the cargo of beauties appeared in splendour as the gallants congregated on the church steps waiting to greet them. They received proposals from gentlemen known and unknown. The greater part of the group was disposed of quickly. What was left of the 'fishing fleet' sailed on to the mofussil to scoop up husbands from the bunch of unmarried officials, planters and businessmen. With such a multitude of wife-seekers, a woman had to be very ugly or over-ambitious not to make her catch and join the 'returned empties', a term used for those returning to England without husbands. The poet Thomas Hood was so struck by this traffic that he satirized the ambitious husband-hunter:

By Pa and Ma I'm daily told
To marry now's my time,
For though I'm very far from old,
I'm rather in my prime
They say while we have any sun
We ought to make our hay
And India has so hot a one
I'm going to Bombay . . .

The girls were advised by their parents not to dance with anyone below the rank of a first class civilian or military officer who could provide three essential things for the happiness of conjugal life in India: a massive silver teapot, a palanquin and a set of bearers to use by day, and a carriage in which to drive in the evening. Following such advice, a girl would sometimes foolishly refuse a really eligible wooer whom she would not have dreamt of finding in England and succumb to the advances of some old nabob with spindle legs. The young civilian was considered a prime catch, 'Pound Sterling 300 a year dead or alive'. The John Company provided an allowance of Pound Sterling 300 a year on marriage to a civilian and on his death a pension for the same amount to the widow. Under the circumstances, it is hardly surprising that girls adopted a somewhat mercenary attitude to the whole matrimonial procedure which is reflected in their letters and journals.

Here is an extract from the 'Lays of Ind', a collection of comic verse which ran into several editions in the last century:

I do believe in dress and ease,
And fashionable dash.
I do believe in bright rupees,
And truly worship cash.
But I do believe that marrying
An acting man is fudge;
And so do not fancy anything
Below a 'pucca' judge.
I do believe that if I'm smart,
And do not lose my head
And cut that thing that's called the heart,
I may fortune wed.

The Indian marriage market excited the imagination and ambition of generations of British girls. It was not unusual for a young girl to marry someone twice or even thrice her age. 'India is a paradise of middle-aged gentlemen', wrote a lady from Madras in 1837; this was because young men in India 'are thought nothing of being posted in remote areas to make or mar their fortunes; but at forty, when they are "high in the service", rather yellow, and somewhat grey, they begin to be taken notice of, and are called "youngmen".' Most often the husbands were hardworking civilians or army officers much older than their wives.

Notices of marriages were inserted in the Calcutta papers such as: 'The marriage is announced of H. Meyer Esq. aged sixty-four to Miss Casina Coupers, a very accomplished young lady of 16 after a courtship of five years.'

Here is another one from a young man in search of a wife.

A young man of Genteel Connexions and Pleasing Appearance, being desirous of providing himself with an Amiable Partner and Agreeable Companion for life, takes this opportunity to solicit the fair hand of a Young and Beautiful Lady: personal accomplishments are absolutely necessary, though fortune will be no object, as he is on the point of taking a long and solitary journey to a distant and remote part of the country, and is anxiously solicitous to obtain a partner of his pleasures and soother of his woes. A line addressed to Mr Atall, No. 100, Writers' Buildings, will meet with every possible attention and the greatest secrecy will not only be observed, but Mr Atall will have the pleasure of giving due encouragement to their favour. Calcutta.
The 21st November 1808

Girls betrothed in England also came to India after years of waiting for their fiancés but this did not always lead to happy reunions. Sometimes the man no longer found the girl attractive and dropped her or if he had got married in the meantime would convey his apologies and offer her all assistance in getting another husband. There were also occasions when the girl after meeting someone on the voyage would have a change of heart and announce on arrival to the waiting aspirant that the engagement was off.

One also comes across some amusing instances of matrimony. There was a colonel in Madras who got married in January and was presented with his first born in March! Another officer was cashiered for seducing an unmarried girl and then arranging her marriage with a brother officer. An officer in Bengal married a woman who had been kept successively by three other army officers. The most extraordinary case, however, was that of Sir Paul Joddrel, physician to the Nawab of Arcot. He lived in Madras with his wife, a young niece by the name of Miss Cummings, and a child. After he had fixed the wedding of Miss Cummings with one Capt. Carlisle, it came to be known that the young one was Sir Paul's mistress, a fact with which Lady Joddrel was well acquainted, and that the child was Sir Paul's by Miss C.

The demand for wives was so great that ladies who lost their husbands had no difficulty in replacing them. A widow was frequently proposed on the steps of the church after the burial of her husband. These speedy marriages were far from uncommon and there were even cases where a wife would engage herself to a suitor during her husband's illness.

The following 'poem' is addressed to a young widow:

What pity, dear widow, that bosom, those eyes,
Should be spoiled—these with weeping, the other with
sighs;
For sighs, like to wind in a bladder, will swell ye.
And tears will but furrow your cheeks, I can tell ye.

Ah, why should you grieve thus, and pleasure forgo
For a husband who died a full twelvemonth ago?
Now, custom prescribes you should make no more
pother;
Forget your first 'Hubby', and choose you another.

Lt. M. Calvert of Madras described his marriage thus: 'A widow came with a daughter who married a Captain and I have married the mother. She is a woman endowed with qualifications that might make any man happy—at least she does me.'

As time passed, more and more memsahibs appeared on the scene as supporting stars in the great imperial drama. With their sense of confidence and power, social life look on a new character.

The memsahibs inculcated a feeling of racial superiority and by the middle of the nineteenth century, liaisons with Indian women were frowned upon and concubinage was morally outlawed. After the Mutiny, the practice virtually died out. By the late 1860s the phenomenon of the 'fishing fleet' was almost over. Metropolitan cities like Calcutta, Bombay and Madras no longer had surplus eligible bachelors pining for nice English girls to replace their native mistresses. The Suez Canal which opened in 1869 shortened the distance between Britain and India by 4,000 miles. It was now easy for young bachelors to go home in three or four years in search of suitable wives.

By the end of the nineteenth century the British had established a chain of civil and military stations and their social life came to revolve within the community. They had their exclusive clubs for entertainment and enjoyment. As to their sex life, it is difficult to determine the truth in the accusation that they committed adultery without compunction.

At home, the Victorian standard of morality was quite strict. There was a general impression that British society in India was immoral and women were the target of most of the criticism. It was believed that husbands and wives spent long periods of time apart from each other, giving opportunities for extramarital affairs.

Flirting with the other sex was a normal part of life in India and married women often attracted hordes of young sparks starved of female company. The fashionable and the indiscreet among them were given amusing nicknames like 'Turban Conquest', 'Betty Bed-and-Breakfast' etc. Hill stations offered plenty of opportunities for fun to lonely wives and civil and military men on leave. There was said to be a hotel in one of the hill stations where the manager rang a bell in the morning to warn his guests to return to their own beds.

Surrounded all the time by servants who noticed their every move the sahibs found that their open lifestyle in a close-knit community gave ample scope for rumours, gossip and scandals. It appeared that the only way in India to keep adultery a secret was to commit it in a moving train! In any event the sahibs' affairs were of little consequence, and did not in any way impair the prestige of the Raj.

The social interaction between the British and the Indians was marked by three distinct phases. The early adventurers who had come to make a fortune cultivated the ruling classes to win commercial contracts, and once established in their various trades developed contacts with the native gentry. This period saw much social intermingling between the two. With the East India Company graduating from a trading venture to a political force, there was a change in attitudes. Social relations gave place to power equations. The situation deteriorated further during the first half of the nineteenth century when the British, who were now the rulers, kept the Indians at a greater distance. The relationship had changed into one of master and servant. The Mutiny swept away what little social intercourse had existed between the two races. Among all the foreigners who successively invaded India, the British alone retained their separate identity, living as exiles until they finally left the country.

William Hickey and
His Bibi Jemdanee

This story is taken from the Memoirs of William Hickey, *one of the world's great diarists and a born storyteller. A famous Calcutta attorney and leading socialite of his days, he presents in, his* Memoirs *a panoramic view of British social life in India during the age of the nabobs in the 1780s and 1790s. Written for his own amusement, the* Memoirs *gives an entertaining account of his personal life as well. Fond of wine and women, a philanderer par excellence, he admits that he 'required no encouragement or any person to show him bad ways, his own evil propensities being quite sufficient'. He relates with realistic detail and remarkable frankness his affairs and encounters with various women. The death of his beloved mistress, Charlotte Barry, brings him the utmost grief, temporarily deadening his senses. However, he recovers in due course and finds solace in the arms of his favourite Indian bibi, the devoted Jemdanee. Respected and admired by his friends, Jemdanee is lauded by Hickey as being 'as gentle and affectionately attached a girl as ever man was blessed with'.*

Hickey had at a very early age begun visiting taverns and brothels in the company of elderly gentlemen. His maiden sexual encounter was with a pretty, smart girl named

1

Nanny Harris who was engaged in his house as a servant and companion to his sisters. In Hickey's words, 'Nanny Harris at once became my delight and I was no less so hers. Every night when the servant had taken away the candle, she used to take me to her bed, there fondle and lay me upon her bosom; nor shall I forget my sensations, infant as I was, at awaking one morning and finding myself snugly stowed between her legs, with one of my hands upon the seat of love, where I have no doubt she had placed it, for she was as wanton a little baggage as ever existed. The early intercourse I had with her strongly influenced me through several years of my life and materially operated in fixing my attachment to women of loose and abandoned principles.'

Hickey recounts his numerous other encounters with maidservants and whores and takes pride in mentioning one of them who 'gave me great credit for my vigour, saying I was a famous little fellow, and should prove an unavoidable acquisition to whatever girl was lucky enough to fix me ... This kind and generous creature I occasionally visited for several years after and sometimes met her accidentally in the streets, when she always addressed me as "her dear little maidenhead". I ever found in her the most sincere and affectionate attachment, and received from her the best advice relative to my future intercourse with her sex'. Even as a boy, Hickey was petted and indulged by some of the fashionable kept women who were unfaithful to their immediate patrons, always having one or more other gallants. Among this class he speaks about a woman of beauty and elegant manners, Fanny Hartford, 'a finer woman in every respect could not be. With her I became so great a favourite that she never was happy unless I was with her'. She later married a gentleman of fortune and settled in countryside.

Hickey then recapitulates one occasion when he went in pursuit of a respectable girl, Ann Malton, daughter of his Art teacher, Thomas Malton. The teacher guessed his plan and thwarted it. Hickey describes how he was exposed and caught redhanded by the father. 'I at first contented myself with occasionally snatching a kiss from her delicious ruby lips, a freedom never strongly opposed and soon, on the contrary, met on her part with the utmost ardour ... The liberties she allowed me to take with her person increased; and I was more than once upon the point of accomplishing the grand object, when her terror lest we should be discovered by some of the servants alone prevented it, and she proposed during the next moonlight night to admit me to her bed ... I advanced, approached the bed and got into it, but had scarcely encircled the object I sought within my arms and our panting bosoms met, when, oh dreadful sound! I heard the door open violently and here I had time to jump out of bed and reach the passage, the father stood before me, dressed with a lighted candle in his hand. Never can I forget the pang I endured at that moment.'

Another affair which Hickey narrates with some fervour is with Emily Warren who dazzled him with her grace, beauty and perfect figure. She was the mistress of his dearest friend Bob Pott. The attachment to her *de facto* husband was however no bar to her amours and Hickey also had no scruple to sleep with her in the absence of his friend, especially after Emily had devoured him with kisses on their very first meeting.

After years of dissipation, we finally find Hickey getting passionately attached to Charlotte Barry whom he manages to steal from Capt. Mordaunt. She declined his offer of marriage but agreed to assume his name and came over with him to India in 1782 as his 'wife'. Here she died in 1783. Hickey was overwhelmed with grief and truly mourned his loss. As he writes, 'Safely may I say, I truly, fondly loved her, with an affection that every new day, if possible, strengthened.' The loss of Charlotte cut short his youth and he took to excessive drinking 'in a hope of drowning reflection and brooding over my misfortune'. After recovering from this emotional depression, he finally yielded to the temptation of wooing native beauties.

'Having from my earliest youth been of an amorous disposition, I began to feel the effects of a long continence. I therefore one night sent for a native woman, but the moment I lay myself down upon the bed all desire ceased, being succeeded by disgust. I could think of nothing but her I had for ever lost, and the bitter recollection rendered me so miserable that I sent off my Hindostanee companion untouched. The same circumstance occurred to me three successive times. Nature, however, at last proved too powerful to be surmounted, and I subsequently ceased to, feel the horror that at first prevailed at the thoughts of a connection with black women, some of whom are indeed very lovely, nor is it correct to call them black, those that come from the Upper Provinces being very fair.'

Hickey goes on to tell us about his mistress Kiraun whom he dismissed after having caught her with one of his servants.

'My friend, Bob Pott,' Hickey writes, 'now consigned to me from Moorshedabad (sic) a very pretty little native girl, whom he recommended for my own private use. Her name was Kiraun. After cohabiting with her a twelvemonth she produced me a young gentleman whom I certainly imagined to be of my own begetting, though somewhat surprised at the darkness of my son and heir's complexion; still that surprise did not amount to any suspicion of the fidelity of my companion. Young Mahogany was therefore received and acknowledged as my offspring, until returning from the country one day quite unexpectedly, and entering Madam Kiraun's apartments by a private door of which I had a key, I found her closely locked in the arms of handsome lad, one of my *kitmuddars*, with the infant by her side, all three being in a deep sleep, from which I awakened the two elders. After a few questions I clearly ascertained that this young man had partaken of Kiraun's personal favours jointly with me from the first month of her residing in my house, and that my friend Mahogany was fully entitled to the deep tinge of skin he came into the world with, being the produce of their continued amour. I consequently got rid of my lady, of her favourite, and the child, although she soon afterwards from falling into distress became a monthly pensioner of mine, and continued so during the many years I remained in Bengal.'

At long last, in 1787, Hickey finds a devoted and affectionate companion in Jemdanee, a charming and sweet-tempered Indian girl. 'I had often admired a lovely Hindostanee girl who sometimes visited Carter at my house, who was very lively and clever. Upon Carter's leaving Bengal I invited her to become an inmate with me, which she consented to do, and from that time to the day of her death Jemdanee, which was her name, lived with me, respected and admired by all my friends for her extraordinary sprightliness and good humour. Unlike the women in general in Asia she never secluded herself from the sight of strangers; on the contrary, she delighted in joining my male parties, cordially joining in the mirth which prevailed, though she never touched wine or spirits of any kind.'

Hickey's extraordinary attachment to Jemdanee is borne out by many affectionate and touching references showing his concern about her health, comforts and happiness. He also delights in narrating various details and incidents of their life together over the years.

In the summer of 1791 Hickey hired a garden house, named 'The White Lion' by his friends, in the cool and pleasant surroundings near a river.

'My Jemdanee was so pleased with the novelty of the thing that nothing would satisfy her but remaining there entirely. She therefore sent for her establishment and settled herself in our upper rooms.

I preferred Calcutta, except on a Saturday night and Sunday, when I sometimes slept in the country. After residing there a fortnight or upwards Jemdanee sent me word she was extremely ill. Ordering my carriage, I immediately went down and found her with a considerable degree of fever, and all her servants more or less indisposed with aguish complaints. Taking her to town, I sent for Doctor Hare, who said it arose entirely from the dampness of the night air, which was peculiar to that part of the country in which our house stood, the wind constantly blowing over a large tract of salt marshes. After this report of the doctor's Jemdanee never would go to the Gardens nor did she ever more enter the house. I believe prejudice operated upon my mind, for I never afterwards went there without fancying myself ill, although I invariably returned to town at night.

Jemdanee early in June importuned me to take her on excursion up the river; in consequence of which I hired the necessary boats, etcetera, and we set off, but got no, further than Chinsurah, the chief settlement of the Dutch in Bengal, for she was so delighted with the place that I was induced to take a house there. Upon observing to Jemdanee that she had been equally pleased with the garden house when we first went there, she exclaimed in Hindostanee, "Yes, I liked the White Lion very well until myself and all the servants became ill there; this is quite another thing; see how dry the walls and every part of the building is, no damp or unwholesome air here, and I'm sure it will agree with us all. I'm also sure I never shall tire of Chinsurah." She proved right; it did agree with everybody wonderfully well, nor did she ever tire of the place.

This house turned out quite the reverse to the "White Lion", for the longer we had it the better we liked everything about it. It suited our habits too: Jemdanee became as stout and healthy as she had ever been, and I constantly found myself less liable to spasmodic attacks and less of an invalid altogether at Chinsurah than in Calcutta. Probably the exercise of going from one place to the other was attended with advantage, as it rendered early rising indispensable, and I was always moving about, the rides and drives in every direction about Chinsurah being exceedingly pretty. It was customary with me either to go up on Friday evening, especially during the moonlight nights, or early on Saturday morning, so as to reach Chinsurah by breakfast time, usually returning to Fort William on Monday morning, though I sometimes made longer stays; nor did I ever go alone, always having some companion to partake of my fare.

Captain Colnett of the *King George* Indiaman, who was at this time in Bengal, frequently accompanied me on a Saturday to Chinsurah, with which excursions he was highly pleased. He soon became a great friend of my favourite Jemdanee's who was fond of romping with her *Lumbah sahib* (big man) as she facetiously called him, he being uncommonly small in stature, certainly not above four feet and a half. He, however, made up in spirit what he wanted in body, for a braver man never existed.'

Jemdanee, affectionately called 'Fatty', was a great favourite with Hickey's friends, who gave her gifts of French jewellery and sent her affectionate messages. One of them, Ben Mee, writing from Europe, trusts that 'Jemdanee has regained her natural spirits and increased to her usual plumpness, both of which so well and so peculiarly become her ... Tell her the first Persian letter I write shall be addressed to the best of all Bibee Sahebs.' In another letter he writes, 'My love and good wishes to the gentle and every way amiable Fatty. Would that her good natured countenance and sweet temper were here. She should have a capital fire in lieu of your burning sun, and nice highly peppered curries!'

Hickey continued his weekly visits to Chinsurah, where his favourite Jemdanee resided almost entirely. 'Her health had materially declined, so much so that for several months I was seriously alarmed, as without any ascertainable or fixed disease she suddenly and rapidly fell away, lost her appetite and her spirits, and seemed to me to be in a quick decline. Conceiving the situation of the house she inhabited might be the cause, I twice changed, and towards the close of the year had the pleasure to see her perfectly restored to health, and once more become fat and cheerful.

In December, I was nominated as Deputy Sheriff, the duties of which office required much of my personal attendance: consequently my excursions to Chinsurah were less frequent; I, however, generally contrived to spend part of Saturday and the whole of Sunday there in the company of my lively girl. From my being so much less there than formerly, she complained of the immense size of the house she inhabited, wishing to have a smaller; to gratify her therefore I hired one upon a more limited scale, at the entrance of the town, and part of it projecting over the river Hooghley. Upon the top of this mansion I built a bungalow, which from its elevated situation was one of the coolest bedchambers in Bengal. Slight as was the construction of this room it cost me upwards of one thousand sicca rupees building. Jemdanee was highly delighted with it.

Finding my health so precarious as to render my existence from month to month very doubtful, and being desirous of making some sort of provision for my favourite Jemdanee, I resolved to build a comfortable habitation for her, and as she entreated that it might be at Chinsurah, I purchased a piece of ground at that place, in a delightful situation, being within a hundred yards of the river, and on the skirts of a beautiful park, in which the Dutch Governor's mansion was. The foundation was laid on the 1st January, 1796, and on the 15th of the following June, to the inexpressible surprise of the inhabitants of Chinsurah, I slept in it completed: but as I had supplied Aumeen, which was the builder's name, with cash whenever he required it, he employed a great number of workmen, executing the job in a very masterly and capital style. This building, including furniture, did not cost me less than forty thousand sicca rupees.

In the month of April 1796, Jemdanee announced to me that she was in a family way, expressing her earnest desire that it might prove "a *chuta* William Saheb".

In August it was my doom to experience another domestic affliction which affected me more than anything which had occurred since losing my dear and ever-lamented Charlotte. My cheerful and sweet-tempered Jemdanee who, from the time of her announcing to me her being pregnant, had gone on admirably well, regularly increasing in bulk, continued in the best state of health, but as I was anxious she should have the medical assistance of a gentleman I placed the utmost confidence in, to attend at the important period of her delivery, I took her from Chinsurah to Calcutta on the 30th of July. Upon our arrival in town I sent for Doctor Hare, who after questioning and examining her apart, told me her confinement might be hourly expected. She remained in uninterrupted health and the highest flow of spirits until the 4th of August when, having laughed and chatted with her after my breakfast, I went to the Court House to attend to a case of considerable importance which was to be tried that morning. I had not been there more than an hour when several of my servants in the utmost alarm ran over to tell me that the Bibee Sahib was dying. Instantly going home, I found my poor girl lying in a state of insensibility, apparently with a locked jaw, her teeth being so fast clenched together that no force could separate them. She had just been delivered of a fine, strong, healthy-looking male child which was remarkably fair.

Doctor Hare arrived in five minutes after I got home, and was greatly surprised and alarmed at the state in which he found her, for which he could in no way account. By the application of powerful drugs which the Doctor administered, she, in half an hour, recovered her senses and speech, appeared very solicitous to encourage and comfort me, saying she had no doubt but she should do very well. Doctor Hare also gave me his assurance that the dangerous paroxysm was past and all would be as we could wish. With this comfortable assurance I again went to attend to my business in Court, from whence I was once more hastily summoned to attend to my dying favourite, who had been suddenly attacked by a second fit from which she never recovered, but lay in a state of confirmed apoplexy until nine o'clock at night when she, without a pang, expired.

Thus did I lose as gentle and affectionately attached a girl as ever man was blessed with. She possessed a strong natural understanding, with more acuteness and wit than is usually to be found amongst native women of Hindostan; and she being a general favourite with all my intimate friends, her death was very sincerely regretted by many. Some days after her burial, upon my making particular enquiries of her female attendants as to the manner she had been attacked in, I was informed that when the pains of labour first came on, she had cried and moaned extremely, whereupon they, according to the orders I had left, directly sent for Doctor Hare, who unluckily was away from home: that after laying an hour in violent agony, she was safely delivered of a boy, when an old Bengallee woman who officiated as midwife, absurdly took it into her head she would have twins, and therefore eagerly desired her to lay still, for that another child was coming. This so terrified the poor suffering girl, that giving a violent screech, she instantly went into strong convulsions, the sad consequence being what I have already related.

Mrs Turner, the wife of my partner, being herself the mother of a numerous family, felt how entirely unequal I should be to undertaking the care of a young infant. She therefore very considerately and kindly ordered the poor little fellow might be conveyed to her house, where she received him as if her own, procuring a nurse and everything that was requisite for him. All my friends humanely exerted themselves to console me under my affliction, the foremost of whom was Colonel MacGowan, who would take no refusal, but compelled me to accompany him to his hospitable residence at Barrackpore where he at that time commanded, and where he kept me twelve days before he would allow me to quit him and return to the duties of my profession.

In the beginning of May my little boy, who had been from the time of his birth under the kind care of Mrs Turner until about a month prior to the above date, and was grown a lovely child, was suddenly become seriously indisposed, and notwithstanding the professional abilities and indefatigable exertions of Doctor Hare, and of his partner Doctor James Williamson, he, after a severe fever of ten days continuance, departed this life, and thus was I deprived of the only living memento of my lamented favourite Jemdanee.'

Reminiscences of a Half-Caste

Until the early decades of the nineteenth century it was common practice for British men to live with Indian women as husband and wife and raise families. These attachments were regarded as a convenience since marrying a young woman from Britain was a costly venture which few could afford. Children born of such alliances however presented problems. Senior officers sometimes sent them to England for education but on their return to India they were denied covenanted positions by the East India Company in spite of their qualifications. Those with proper contacts landed in the princely states while others were compelled to accept middle level jobs in the Company's civil and military set-up. Unfortunately, they carried with them the stigma of illegitimacy and thus were shunned by the British. The majority of natives too treated them as outcastes of low social origin.

The source of this story is The East India Sketch-Book *series (4 vols) by a 'Lady', published in 1832 and 1833. It contains lively accounts of British social life in the Presidency towns of Calcutta, Bombay and Madras as well as in other smaller stations and cantonments. The anonymous author in her introduction describes India as 'the land of enchantment—the treasure house from which imagination culls its brightest images of splendour—the golden orient glittering in the best brilliance of sun and song'. Besides depicting the pattern of life and the local scene, the author narrates a number of true-to-life incidents, some of which portray the status of children born of Indian mothers and European fathers. 'The Reminiscences of a Half-Caste' is one such episode which recalls the racial prejudices and other hardships faced by a young Eurasian.*

I mourned over my departure from England. It was a first class ship and the number of passengers was great. There were some individuals amongst us distinguished if not for brilliancy, at least for length of service, and to these the name of General Vane was familiar, and to a few evidently that of an intimate. Yet they extended little notice to his son and a thousand minute circumstances made me feel that my position was equivocal and mysterious even to myself. I felt intimately that there was some inexplicable degradation connected with me, but the straining of every faculty of my mind did not aid me on discovering whence it originated until Storemont, a young cavalry officer who looked on me with compassion, revealed to me my true position. 'My dear Vane,' said he, 'I cannot sufficiently condemn the system which has allowed you to remain in such complete ignorance of the peculiarities of the Indian services, of the exclusion of all individuals, who are maternally of Asiatic origin, in short, whom we, in our English phraseology, call half-castes.'

Yes, from that moment the mystery was revealed, one word had dissipated the darkness and solved the enigmas of men's coldness to me—I was a half-caste.

On arrival in India, I had no fault to find with the cordiality of General Vane's reception, and yet it did not satisfy me. General Vane's whole manner was that of a friend warmly interested in my behalf, but it was not, even on retrospection I feel that it was not, the manner of a father. No touch of parental emotion affected his voice when he addressed me, or his eye as he gazed on me.

And I had a means of comparison also, a sense of the slender tie which my birth gave me on him, forced on me by his evident fondness for his legitimate, his European offspring.

The cold politeness of the reception vouchsafed me by Mrs Vane, left me no tangible ground of complaint. She was quite as courteous, more indeed than my father's natural son had a right to expect from my father's lawful wife.

General Vane secured for me the position of Lieutenant in the Nizam's service and I joined the duties with the regiment at Bolarum. Under the most favourable circumstances, a military life would never have been my choice. The eternal succession of drills and parades, without 'end or aim'; the restraint to which inclination, habit, even convenience must necessarily be submitted; the implicit obedience to an individual, to whom it was perhaps irksome to pay even the slightest deference of external respect; the complete absence of the necessity of thought and reflection, when the perfection of discipline is the passiveness of a machine; all had a tendency to depress the best aspirations of the mind, and by depriving intellect of any impetus to exertion, to crush its energies. The only alleviation to such an existence would have been the society of congenial companions, and under my unfortunate circumstances, I had no prospect of meeting with such. Those between whom and myself the similar conditions of our birth established an apparent bond of union had generally been educated entirely in India, and were ignorant of even the first elements of European literature, manners and morals. *As a class*, none could be more debased; they seemed animated by a universal desire of justifying the contempt with which they were regarded, and of illustrating in their own persons the truth that they were not only unredeemed, but unredeemable. I could hardly deem it unjust that I was excluded from *equal* association with the higher classes of English officers in my neighbourhood, since the conduct of these of whom I seemed *one* not only exercised but demanded such exclusion. Of the female part of the class, some were the wives of British gentlemen, and to their tables I might have had constant access. In a short time, however, the invitations which, from curiosity, or perhaps the better motive of hoping for the existence of higher virtues amongst female half-castes, I had accepted, were declined as often as common courtesy permitted me to follow the bent of my inclination. Alas, how have I deplored the truth of an assertion so frequently made by the proud youth of unadulterated western origin, that no man can form a union with one of these women without deteriorating in intellect, in morals, in manners! How many an evidence of its correctness might be culled from the annals of private life in India.

The only flower that bloomed in the desert of my existence was the access I found to the domestic society of Colonel Hargrave, then commanding the Hyderabad force. A letter from General Vane had first obtained for me the honour of his notice, and possibly the circumstances of my English education, and the turn of mind and thought consequent on the long period I had spent in Europe, under the influence of prospects likely to extend its duration through my life, secured its continuance. Never can I recall the hours spent in his house, even before the time when they became so, inexpressibly dear to me without feelings of the deepest gratitude. Yes, blighted as all my hopes are, and proceeding in some measure from *his* hand as the wreck of all my dearest affections has done, I cannot but do justice to a man so deserving of the highest reverence. A brave soldier, an accomplished gentleman, an honourable man, a pious Christian—what a union of admirable qualities! Unblemished himself and so lenient in his judgement of the errors of others; so intellectual, and yet so tolerant of the dullness to which he was daily exposed, so admirable an officer, yet so forbearing when the offence was of no graver character than the waywardness of youth, or the infirmity of nature, so dignified, yet gentle in rebuke, so warm and sincere in praise—never in my path through fife, have I seen the man of whom I could say, *he* transcends the excellence of Colonel Hargrave.

He loved England, but prudence compelled his prolonged sojourn in India, and when I was first introduced to his acquaintance, Mrs Hargrave was daily expected to return from England with their only daughter, whose guardianship had been the object of her voyage home.

They arrived, the mother and daughter. She, Helen Hargrave, was an inmate in the house of her father. Redolent with all the graces of youth and joy, pure of heart and holy in feeling, as those should be who are nurtured in the island home of the west; beautiful as the morning star, refreshing as the morning dew, innocent of all the prejudices imbibed in the East; hardly conscious of any distinction between man and man, except as between ignorance and knowledge, vulgarity and intellect, baseness and honour; she beamed upon my path as a light from heaven which could never lead astray.

How long, deeply, I loved her, before I was even dreaming of the nature of the attachment she excited! I wrapped my spirit in the delusion that my gratitude for the friendship and countenance of Colonel Hargrave not only permitted, but demanded, that I should look on his daughter with feelings far deeper than ordinary mortals are wont to excite. Alas! I suspected not that already to *me* Helen Hargrave stood out in her individual self as apart from, and unconnected with, all besides in this lower world; that, as far as regarded *her*, the existence of her father was never remembered by me; that the deep, the absorbing sentiment *she* had excited, was wholly distinct from every other feeling that had affected my soul; that gratitude, friendship, all faded, withered beneath its intense power. Except in her presence, all existence was to me a memory and a hope. The present *was not*. My consciousness dwelt on what she had said and done, or my expectation on what she was yet to do. Love in its purest burning idolatry, engrossed me; *undivided first love*.

Absorbed in the ardour of my passion, I never contemplated its ultimate results. I had no thought for a remote future. I had surrendered my whole being so completely to the influence of Helen, that I had not even analysed what precise effect I contemplated from our present uncontrolled intercourse. Satisfied with the intense enjoyment which the daily sight of her imparted, the possibility of our separation had not, for a moment, darkened my spirit. If I had indulged any definite hope of making her wholly and absolutely my own, that would have had the effect of rousing me to a sense of the reality of the circumstances which surrounded me. The attentions she received from others appeared an homage naturally due to the transcendent graces and excellence that enthralled me. Her courtesy to her father's guests never defrauded me of her sweetest smile, her softest accents. I had no fear of rivals, because, as I have said, my feelings were vague in everything but their tenderness; I was without jealousy, because I never witnessed in her any exhibitions of preference which, by alarming, would have enlightened me. My love was as unmingled with alloy as any passion that ever warmed the human heart.

It is not surprising that the watchful affection of a mother was the first to awaken to a scene of alarm for the worldly welfare of the one being in whom centred all her cares, all her hopes. If her utter disbelief of the possibility that her daughter's affections *could* decline upon a wretch whose natural inheritance was shame had so long lulled suspicion to sleep, her convictions were but the stronger, and her resolution the more vigorous.

One morning I called at the house of Colonel Hargrave with a collection of Chinese paintings which Helen had expressed a desire of seeing. I found the Colonel alone, and was grieved at the evident depression of spirits which mingled with his kind greeting; beyond this commiseration I was not agitated by one feeling of alarm or apprehension. After sitting a few minutes I enquired for the ladies, and felt somewhat indignant on hearing that they were gone to the Residency for the day, because I was punctual in appearing at the precise hour which Helen herself had appointed for our meeting. I am sure my countenance expressed how much I was disconcerted. Colonel Hargrave rose, and asked me to walk with him into his private apartment.

My heart at that instant first entertained a vague foreboding, that its cup of bliss was to be tasted no more. I obeyed the invitation with a trembling anticipation that I and happiness were about to part for ever. The Colonel closed the door as I entered, and invited me to sit near him.

He was silent for some seconds, apparently unwilling to commence a task enforced on him. He rose, and paced the room several times, whilst my eye was fixed on him, endeavouring to penetrate the workings of his mind. As soon as our glances met, he paused and stood before me.

'Vane,' said he, in a low, subdued voice, 'I have but one child, the hopes, the prospects of the last of a far-descended line centre in her.'

He paused—I held my very breathing in dread of that which was yet to be said.

He paced the apartment again to nerve his resolution, before he addressed me. 'Far be it from me,' he said, 'you will do me the justice to believe it *is* far from me, to mention to you, as matter of reproach, those unfortunate circumstances of your birth, which, whatever they involve, leave you at least guiltless. Unhappily the punishment of error often extends far beyond those who actually perpetrate it. During the period of our intercourse I have sedulously endeavoured to stifle the voice of those prejudices which, you are aware, are entertained by *all* Europeans resident in India, even :by those who are the parents or the partners of-of-half-castes; forgive the term; you know how general is its use here. What shall I say? Do not think that I am tender of myself in this distressing business. Believe me, I feel that if an impartial person were to sit in judgement on all those concerned in the matter, I should probably be deemed the most culpable. Even now perhaps—but no; you, Vane, at least will not think my interference premature; you know well with what sentiments you have regarded my only child!'

I covered my face with my hands, as if, in daring to lift up my eyes—my hopes—to the pure and lovely object of my idolatry, I had committed an offence for which I ought to blush even in the presence of her father!

'Be not distressed,' he resumed; 'I interpret your silence, as if to any but one blind as myself there needed other interpreters than your looks, your language, for weeks past! How could it have been otherwise? Was it in youth and intellect to associate constantly, daily, with Helen Hargrave, and to remain insensible to all those graces and endowments, which make her the pride of her father? In one word, Vane, you love, and Helen—it is sufficient, that, for both your sakes, you must meet no more!'

I looked up at him with a strange mingling of feelings. Why, in that moment of despair, was I sensible to the ecstasy of being beloved by Helen?—of understanding from her father's avowal that a creature so bright, so gifted, participated in the love which devoured me?

'Yes,' he repeated calmly, 'Helen Hargrave and you must meet no more! Nurtured as I have been in all the, perhaps faulty, prejudices of birth, were you possessed of all the treasures of the East, you never could be the husband of my child! It is not my wish unnecessarily to afflict you, but, for *her* sake, for yours, it behoves me to speak explicitly. I would not give my daughter to the unlawful son of the proudest monarch of the earth! And, in the *double* stigma which the conventions of society attach to—my poor boy, check this afflicting agitation!—believe that you are not the only person who requires pity now!'

I endeavoured to subdue my emotions, and perhaps a proud thought that, in my own peculiar individuality, I was not altogether unworthy of Helen, might not have been utterly scorned by her father, aided me to regain the appearance of composure. As soon as I was able, I hastened to speak.

'I acknowledge the justice of your decision. Colonel Hargrave,' I said, 'there exists not on the earth a being more deeply sensible than myself of the inexpiable stain that attends my birth—I was but lately awakened to a consciousness of it. In the happier years of my youth, in the home where I was so carefully cherished in England, I felt not, dreamed not, the extent of the degradation to which I was born. That I *have* loved—that I *do* love—your daughter passionately, fondly, purely, I will not deny; it will be the pride of my future life that I was not insensible to those high endowments which exalt her so immeasurably above the rest of her sex. And yet, Colonel, in having lifted up my thoughts to her, I can hardly charge myself with presumption. So vague have been all my wishes, that I am not conscious whether at any one moment I fostered the vain hope of making her my wife. Satisfied with the enjoyment of her society, occupied by the absorbing delight of the present, I think I may assert that I never extended my views beyond the passing hour. If I *had* tutored my mind to more definite expectations, perhaps this interference, which I am sure is painful to you, would have been unnecessary. Yes! believe me, I myself should have been the first to prevent her degradation; to have shielded her from participation in those unnumbered stings which render *my* existence a succession of pains. Miss Hargrave, Colonel, has nothing to fear from my pursuit; I shall carefully abstain from the indulgence of even a casual encounter with her. May she be happy in a union with one, whose name may bestow on her all the honour she can ever receive from any worldly distinction!'

Colonel Hargrave clasped my hand. Alas! at that moment I could have spared such an evidence of his gratitude for the sacrifice I was offering up of the purest, the fondest, attachment that ever animated a human heart! 'I thank you,' said he, 'With a father's deepest gratitude I thank you! If Heaven had permitted that you had been of any origin but— but—*this*, I would have welcomed my son-in-law, as one whose alliance could have brought me only honour! As it is, it remains for me only to assure you, that you have in me a firm friend, who will exert his warmest efforts for your advantage; and to fulfil my pledge to Helen, that, before you departed, I would place this unopened in your hands.'

He gave me a small, sealed packet. Hardly making a sign of farewell, I returned to my own house, and securing my chamber, opened the last token I ever received of *her* existence. It was her own writing. I knew every flowing line of that delicate autograph. Long the letters swam in indistinctness before my eyes, and it was with a dizzy brain, a mind almost bewildered, that I read as follows:

'My father has not opposed my desire—*my prayer*—to bid you a long farewell—a *farewell* of which no hope of future meeting alleviates the bitterness—it is farewell for ever, Walter! Yes, for the first, for the last time, I will address you by a name which my lips have never yet adventured to pronounce! Much as our hearts have overleapt the barriers of society, at least we have restrained our speech to all the formality of its requirements. But now—now—in *this* moment surely the iron boundary of social conventions may be passed. Whilst I *feel* that you are *Walter*, I will call you so, above the whisper of my heart, as you, in the depths of yours, have thought of me only as *Helen*!

I was contented in your presence—satisfied with your society, without a thought beyond today, undreaming of the future—until another awakened me to a conviction of the nature of the—what shall I call it?—the preference I was indulging; I knew not that I was standing on the brink of a precipice from which the downward leap was—oh, how fatal! I have never heard from you the words, '*I love you, Helen!*' and yet must I write to you as if all between us had been revealed by the ordinary methods of human intercourse. What need of declaration when all was so well understood without it. You will not entrench yourself in pride behind this poor evasion will you, Walter? You will not say, the poor Helen was all too forward in interpreting actions and looks which signified nothing but cold esteem for her father's daughter. No, my heart will not imagine such a treachery, and turns with impatience from the fears of my mother, which tremble for the possible humiliation of her child!

Doubtless we shall be unhappy, Walter, but let the same thought fortify *your* soul as supports mine: we have done no wrong, we have betrayed no trust; if we have fallen into error, it was through ignorance of the abyss towards which our footsteps were wandering. We part for ever, and in this obedience to the mandates of imperative duty, we earn the only alleviation of which the pain of such a separation is susceptible. We cannot condemn, even in this our first agony, the resolution of my father; you, as well as I, are sensible of the impossibility of our permanent union. Alas! what has he to answer for, whose sin thus is the commencing point of a series of humiliations and sufferings, that must in a degree track the existence of the being called into existence by a father's crime!

Forgive—forgive, Walter, every word that can wound or depress you! You know that there are few sufferings I would not undergo to spare you an hour's anguish. Pity the occasional bitterness of spirit which *will* display itself, when all that is too vividly contrasted with all that *might have been*!

My letter has but one ostensible object, and yet I have written thus long without touching on it. I do not bid you forget me, but to think of me often, and with *kindness*. Love is crushed for ever from the pathway of my existence; may yours be more blessed! By the remembrance of all the hours we have spent together, I adjure you not to spurn the offers which my father's billet will submit to you. Let no false pride lead you to reject a kindness, which inflicts on him who proffers it neither privation nor inconvenience. Reflect, that it is not Colonel Hargrave, but *the father of Helen* whose exertions are to place you in a sphere more congenial to your habits and tastes than this strange world of India. Do not—do not add to my cup the only additional drop which can augment its bitterness. Ere you reject, think that you are about to tear away the last illusion of hope which lingers about the existence of *Helen*.'

How often this farewell was read, how wept over, it boots not to think on. There was a short note accompanying it, which for hours was suffered to lie unheeded on my desk. When I opened it, I comprehended the extent of Helen's anxieties that I should not spurn the kindness of her father.

'Helen's note my dear young friend, will have convinced you that, however imperative may have been the causes which have compelled me to separate you, personal dislike was the sentiment the farthest in the world from mingling with them. If the sense of individual merit could, in any case, have led me to disregard the first—perhaps the most rational—of social prejudices, it would have done so in the instance which is at present inflicting so much pain on all of us. Believe that next to the welfare of my child, *yours* is the first wish of my heart; and in saying thus much, I feel myself bound, by every means in my power, to promote it. Your education, your prolonged residence in England, your peculiar tastes, combine to render India the place in the world least likely to afford you such happiness as may be reasonably expected in the course of human existence. My interest in England has been so long dormant, from the absence of any efficient stimulus to its exertion, that I have a long arrear of claims on the favourable attention of many influential persons at home. I have sufficient influence with General Vane to ensure his approbation of your proceeding immediately to

Calcutta on leave, of your subsequent resignation of the Nizam's service, and consequent embarkation for England. His paternal desire for your happiness and respectability, both of which will I am confident, be materially advanced by this step, will be a powerful motive with him to advance the funds necessary to enable you to adopt this plan. I shall not so far anticipate his refusal, as to say, that should it occur, I at least will be ready to meet all your wants. The General may have erred—may be severe—but in this instance I venture to assert that he will be *just*. He will rejoice in the certainty of such a position for you in England as will place you in a rank befitting *his son*, and secure such a permanent provision as cannot be calculated on from the chances of the service to which you are at present attached. May you enjoy all the happiness your high qualities so abundantly merit!'

Yes, Helen read me rightly. My first resolution was an indignant refusal to accept aught from him who withheld from me all I coveted on earth. Helen! the sacrifice of pride, at least, was deserved by thee, and it was made!

I am at Calcutta. Even now yonder vessel has weighed anchor, and is dropping about for her passengers. Another hour, and I shall have left for ever the land in which every blessed vision of youth has melted away! With a spirit bowed down by incessant humiliations, a heart seared by the most bitter disappointment, a judgement warped by the constant sense of suffering for the crime of another, a spirit indignant at those conventions of society which reason nevertheless pronounces most hallowed—whatever may be my subsequent fate, whatever my future elevation, shall I for one moment forget that the burning brand of shame has marked me—that I am under the withering curse of illegitimacy—a half-caste!

Revenge of the Native Mistress

The early English settlers were generally much influenced by Indian customs and manners. It was common practice for the sahibs to set up zenanas or keep native mistresses. However, from the 1830's onwards, when British women started arriving in India in increasing numbers, such liaisons came to be frowned upon. Tender and lasting in many cases, these relationships were born of necessity. Gradually, the social pressure of the memsahibs had its way in driving out the Indian mistresses from the English households. Contemporary writings, especially by some women authors, portray Indian bibis in a negative light, dubbing them wicked and selfish. Young newcomers were advised to shun their company and not fall prey to their charms.

This story highlighting the tragic consequences of one such relationship is taken from The East India Sketch-Book *series (1832-33) written by an anonymous woman writer.*

Wilmer was the second son of a German Baron of sixteen quarterings. Nothing, perhaps, could have counteracted effectually the Baron's pride of plunging into the unfathomable abyss of genealogy, in the depths of which lay his own antiquity of origin, but the symptoms of approaching starvation, which the empty butteries and unroofed galleries of his dilapidated ancestral castle exhibited.

27

Precisely at the same epoch there was living and fattening on the good things of this world, a person who united in himself every characteristic most decidedly opposite to those which distinguished the Baron; nevertheless these contrasts were the children of the same parents. How and why the younger should have emigrated from the neighbourhood of Stralsburg to London—how he prospered there, and attained wealth, and its concomitant, influence, it is not necessary to inquire here. The Baron's dignity had, in former days, cut the connection, but the Baron's poverty was too glad to renew it when a provision for his unfriended sons was a matter of inevitable necessity. Pride affected to make conditions as to the mode in which wealth was to contribute aid, and stipulated for gentility. The old merchant and director, compassionating his own blood, as he said, overlooked the presumption of the stipulation—adopted his nephew and namesake, Frederick, to his particular favour and especial patronage—sent him as a preliminary measure to the University of Halle, and at nineteen embarked him for India, with the credentials of an Artillery cadetship.

And what did Frederick acquire during his few years of academic life? The classics, perhaps?—or moral or natural philosophy?—or—why waste time in conjecture? He learned love and mysticism; and which had the greater share in transforming the hardy, robust mountaineer into a pale, melancholy, shadowy-looking young man, it might puzzle a metaphysician to determine.

Sophia Sternhof lived just opposite the lodgings of Frederick's great and kind friend, Professor X——. No man was a more devout Kantean than the excellent professor, but he ate and drank like a materialist. So, whilst he slept after dinner, Wilmer occasionally diverted himself by gazing at his vis-a-vis neighbour, because all study, he argued, though it be the fascinating knowledge of transcendentals, requires relaxation. Perhaps the fine display of roses and other flowers in the opposite balcony was his first attraction: no matter, there was cause and effect, and very soon Wilmer saw amongst those flowers only the combination of all their graces in Sophia. All the world knew that Madame Sternhof was a cripple; her misfortune was the result of a long attendance on this only child during a very severe and threatening malady. She was a widow, and she was poor; her circumstances and her malady conduced equally to her seclusion. Sophia was never to be seen in the places of public resort; she was a violet blooming the more sweetly for the shade that embosomed her, for she caught only the first and the last rays of the sun in retired walks before Madame Sternhof rose in the morning, or during her afternoon's siesta.

Sophia was a German, but her features and complexion were not national. She had the darkest hair and eyes, an oval face, features of Grecian outline, and a fair pale cheek, resulting perhaps as much from confinement and circumstances as from constitution. She was tall, but her perfect proportions gave her figure the most feminine elegance, and her step was light and sylph-like. She was often occupied amongst the roses of her balcony, and though at first she retired, on perceiving to what point the intense gaze of the student was directed, she became used to it at length, and, in short, it was not long before he walked by her side during her evening airings, and a few months were sufficient to plunge them into the depths of a pure and first attachment. The Lombard-street Wilmer required the immediate presence of his nephew in London. The cadetship awaited his arrival, and—and in short the one great conviction on the mind of Frederick was. thousands of leagues of land and ocean were about to divide him from Sophia—for ever!

Yes, for ever! In his despair, the distance and the time seemed extended beyond human calculation. It was infinity—it was eternity—a future of darkness, whether in life or death, mysterious and unknown.

He did, for a moment, indulge the wish—the hope—that Sophia would accompany him to the far-off world for which he was destined. One word from her was sufficient to crush that single blooming hope, to break that one line of light.

Could she desert her mother?—render the widow childless?—the poor destitute?—the infirm helpless? Wilmer hated himself that he had asked such a sacrifice; a thousand vows were exchanged, hours of pain and agony wept away—and they parted.

His correspondence with Sophia was punctual, but then a weary year must elapse before he could receive her answer to each letter. He loved her fervently, ardently as ever. But his mind was devouring itself. Beyond the reach of access to books, satiated with his own limited store, not only indifferent to, but actually averse to field-sports, existence became daily less tolerable, and he fell into guilt to avoid the horrors of that loneliness which threatened him with the grave.

How a man of cultivated mind and high endowments can descend to a tie with a female whose manners, heart, everything, contain the elements of all that, in theory, most disgusts him, is one of those effects

> In which the burden of the mystery
> Of all this unintelligible world

is, perhaps, felt most bitterly. It is true, Orissa had exceeding beauty, and the grace of form peculiar to Indian women, to attract the senses. There was no suspicion of impurity attached to her till now; she was the orphan of a deceased Subidar, and perhaps Wilmer viewed her as one whom he himself had despoiled. Was he happy in his new connection? Let him answer who, not yet lost to virtue, has foully wronged the one confiding and faithful heart that has trusted its sum of happiness to his keeping, and lives hopefully, if not happily, in the conviction of his unswerving fidelity.

Pain, acute and remorseful, mingled with his expectation of Sophia's letters. There was even a feeling, unacknowledged perhaps to his own heart, a feeling of relief, if they came not. And yet, 'he had not forgotten his first love'. All the worthy tenderness of his heart was fully engrossed by her, but he knew in what he had offended, and he shrank from the close contemplation of the difference between her heart and his, which those letters of pure and devoted affection forced on him.

The brightness of Sophia's prospects in Germany had not increased since they parted. 'My dear mother,' she wrote in one of her letters, 'grows weaker daily. Every morning I think I perceive a diminution of health in her countenance, and the accents of her voice falter when she blesses me. Ah, if it would please God to spare my dear parent to me, I would regret your absence less, Frederick, than I have been wont to do.'—'Dearest Frederick,' said another letter, 'I have been long without writing to you, and I scarcely know why I should write now. I have tried to hide what I feel, and almost think it wrong to cast the shadow of my grief over your path. But indeed, Frederick, I feel my utter loneliness so painfully, that I am driven to write to you, as the only refuge from the sorrows that oppress me.' 'The stroke has fallen,' she wrote again. 'You will grieve for me; my dearest mother died three months since. You will not wonder that I have not written before; indeed I have not had the heart to do so; it seemed to me a treason to her memory to think of any subject connected with hope. But now, I come to you for advice and direction, which our engagement and our affection gives me a right to ask, and you a right to afford. You know the small income on which we formerly subsisted was only a pension for my mother's life—consequently, now it is withdrawn; and the little fund she so carefully accumulated for me, together with the produce of our household furniture, will afford me the means of existence only during a few months. There is, therefore, but a choice of dependence; do you point out such a mode in which my exertions shall be made, as will be least disagreeable to you. My cousin, the banker's wife, at Leipzig, has written to offer me the advantage of her protection, as instructress to her five children. I am going to her directly, and shall await your reply there. I do not think any plan could be more acceptable to you than this; and you will be comforted by knowing that, if I be dependent, it is on my own kinswoman. Besides, life is not all roses.'

'Life is not all roses,' sighed Wilmer, as he finished the last letter. The death of Mrs Sternhof affected him painfully, but the disposal of Sophia was a much more interesting point to be considered. The irrevocable past was beyond his power, and he set himself seriously to decide on his views for the future.

Amidst all the difficulties of the situation in which folly and frailty had placed him, let it not be supposed that Wilmer for a moment hesitated on deciding that his union with Sophia should be effected with all possible speed. A very little calculation sufficed to show, how much less expensive and difficult her coming out to India immediately would be, than his returning to England for the purpose of escorting her. But by far the most difficult task remained; he felt it imperative on him, by honour, principle, even inclination, to dissolve instantly and for ever his unhappy connection. Aware with what too great indulgence this sin is regarded in India, he felt the less reluctance to ask the aid and advice of Captain Aubrey, who commanded the troop of Horse Artillery to which Wilmer had been removed. Captain Aubrey was married, and had offered his house as a residence for Sophia on her arrival, as soon as he heard of Wilmer's project. To him, therefore, Wilmer applied for two months' leave of absence, and to him he resigned the power of terminating a thraldom the yoke of which became every hour more galling.

Wilmer had been absent about a fortnight when he received the following letter from Captain Aubrey:

My dear Wilmer,

In the first place, let me relieve your mind by telling you, you are free. The girl has left your house for ever, I trust. I have disposed of a sum in her behalf, which will produce her ten rupees a month for her life, put out to usury after the native fashion. This will be done by an agent over whom I shall be always able to keep an eye; for, *sub silentio sit*, he belongs to the troop; and depend on it if there is any failure in punctuality on his part, we shall hear of it.

I need not relate to you all my arguments and persuasions, because to me 'nothing so tedious as a twice-told tale'. You may imagine the violence of a native woman, and the superior energy of her language, which, you know, is on no occasion limited by the restraints of common decency. She threatens you with all manner of evil and vengeance; and I hear she was making *pooja* at the Swami's house on the left of our lines, a few nights since, to call down mischief and punishment on you. There is one point on which you may set your mind at ease: Hall recognized her when she visited my verandah the other day; he swears she lived with Jones of the 81st, before she was fourteen; he spoke to her, and she received him with all the ease of an old acquaintance. Her father, it is true, was a Subidar, but a Pariah; he got his promotion in days of yore when we looked less to a Sepoy's caste than now; so, you see, she had no caste to violate. In every respect you are well rid of her, for, setting aside the superior beauty of her person, she is one of the worst of her species I ever happened to meet.

You have suffered so much on account of this unhappy affair, that your own mind has already suggested more admonitions than my lazy pen is likely to afford you. I wish no cadet came out before he was twenty, and every one married. If I had a voice in the legislature, I would vote to establish it by Act of Parliament.

I have concluded, you see, with an opinion worthy of a married man. However, as I hope soon to greet you a member of the fraternity, I need not apologize for sentiments, the justice of which I think you will at this moment most particularly approve.

Ever, my dear Wilmer,

Yours most sincerely,
C. Aubrey

Wilmer was well satisfied that he had thus finally shaken off the trammels of his culpable connection, but he felt some of those uncomfortable misgivings, which invariably attend the commission of wrong. He resolved to remain absent during the whole of his two months' leave, trusting that, the habit of separation once fixed, he should escape future annoyance.

With the pertinacity which distinguishes these unhappy creatures, the discarded woman sometimes found means of approaching Wilmer. In his solitary morning's walk she occasionally presented herself before him with prostration, and tears, and all that is in fact part of the vocation of her class. But when Wilmer, by repeated resistance, proved himself invulnerable, and resigned his early sauntering abroad, her attacks assumed a different character; she came boldly to his house with threats, violence, and outcries, calling down vengeance, and menacing him with the infliction of it. Captain Aubrey's interference was, at first, ineffectual; and it was not until the withdrawing of her stipend for two or three months that she finally retreated, and left Wilmer to comparative tranquillity.

At length one cause of doubt and agitation was removed. He received a letter from Sophia.

'Yes, I am indeed coming to you, dear Frederick; I bring with me, dear Frederick, a heart unchanged in warm affection to you, but, at present, sad and desponding. You will not find my person improved; but if you think me paler and thinner, you will remember that I have passed through some suffering since we parted, and will not love me less for the change. I own, however, that I wish we had once met again and at least resumed our acquaintance.'

At last Sophia was united with her love Wilmer; every anxiety seemed banished from the heart of Sophia, in the fulness of her present happiness. There was the deep and luxurious repose that succeeds tumult and extreme agitation; her hopes were now fully realized. Wilmer, too, felt that happiness was all around him.

One evening, Sophia and Wilmer had strolled through an avenue bounded on either side by plantain and guavas and they now reposed in an open verandah, looking out upon the garden before them. If they sighed at contrasting the oriental character of the scene with their own European home, they felt likewise that they were together, and wished not, asked not, for change.

Aubrey and his wife joined them, and they conversed playfully. Wilmer, for once, seemed to deliver himself up entirely to happiness; he was unusually cheerful, and when Mrs Aubrey afterwards dwelt on that evening, she confessed that Wilmer was so unlike himself, that his vivacity had impressed her mind with a pain almost like an acute pang inflicted on her body.

By degrees Sophia became less animated; but as the others were conversing with great eagerness, her complete abstraction was not at first perceived: Wilmer was the first to be conscious of it, and, looking in her face, his own reflected back its extreme paleness.

'Heavens, Sophia, you are very ill!'

He clasped her hands in his. They were cold and damp. Mrs Aubrey, roused by his evident alarm, rose also: 'My dear Sophia, what is the matter?'

'I do not know; I cannot tell; it was a sudden pang—a faintness—a numbness, a-a—Wilmer! oh, Wilmer!' and she fell back in his arms.

Wilmer was nearly as powerless as his fainting bride. Aubrey took her in his arms and carried her into the house.

He exchanged a look with his wife, that revealed at once all he knew, and all he feared. The nature of the attack was not to be mistaken.

Medical aid was almost instantly administered. Wilmer, scarcely conscious of anything that was occurring, paced the garden, with his hands pressed on his hot brow, gazing upwards with his burning eyes, sensible of pain and anguish, but bewildered wherefore and why.

There were symptoms not to be mistaken; but there were others as inexplicable. 'What I can comprehend of this case,' said the Surgeon to Mrs Aubrey, 'threatens nothing fatal; but there are symptoms apparent that lead me to suspect the illness of our patient to have been produced by causes purely external. Has she eaten anything unusual—anything more than is generally on your table?'

'Nothing. I remember nothing,' said Mrs Aubrey, dreadfully agitated; 'surely, surely, Doctor, you suspect nothing very—that is—'

'We must endeavour to ascertain what has been taken,' he returned evasively: 'I will see Wilmer; perhaps he may be able to elucidate what, I confess, embarrasses me.'

It was some minutes before Wilmer could be made to comprehend the nature of the questions asked by the Surgeon. At length he said he had brought her some bon bons, in the manufacture of which one of his servants was very skilful; that Sophia had frequently before eaten them, without any bad effect, and in larger quantities, for she had reserved a great portion of these for the children.

Doctor V. desired to see what remained.

When they were produced, he examined several closely and minutely. 'Send for your boy,' said he to Wilmer; 'I wish to ask him a question.'

But the boy was no longer to be found; and now that discovery seemed at hand, as is usual with natives of this class, each individual of Wilmer's household had something to disclose of the absentee, which had never before been suspected.

He had been Wilmer's favourite attendant; his dressing boy, always about his person. It now appeared that he had also been so high in the favour of the unfortunate and guilty woman, formerly living with Wilmer, that it was no secret to his fellow-servants that he was her paramour.

Moreover, it was ascertained, that she had, for several days, been lurking in the neighbourhood of Wilmer's compound, that Mootasawny had had repeated interviews with her, and that on one occasion he had gone to sleep before his master's return from Captain Aubrey's at night, being intoxicated—that before he slept he had talked strangely, and had told them, 'Never any good when Mistress come . . . better not let come . . . Master good, quiet gentleman; what for Mistress want? . . . not let come.'

The evidence was more than sufficient to corroborate the suspicions of Doctor V. He was quite sure that some noxious drug or herb had been administered, and with inexpressible grief he was obliged to confess that the disease was beyond the power of his art.

Wilmer admitted the conviction in all its depth of darkness and of horror; Sophia was dying, and link by link he traced the chain of the tragedy to the first moving cause— his own guilt. He was very calm—so calm, that no opposition was made to his being present by the dying couch of Sophia.

The face was fearfully changed; the whole frame was collapsed in a degree that seemed the effect of years of disease, rather than of a few minutes. She smiled gently when she became conscious that Wilmer was near, but generally she lay in a state of quiet, resembling torpor.

Her hand lay in his, passive and cold as if already that of a corpse, except when a convulsive pressure and a correspondent contraction of feature, indicated a spasm of pain. Towards the last her eye gained an expression of strong consciousness. She looked round at Mrs Aubrey, at Aubrey— and smiled peacefully and gratefully. That dark and intellectual eye looked more brightly and tenderly than ever, as it poured its glance of parting love on the one being who had excited the first—the last passion of her pure heart. The lips moved, but 'Wilmer' was scarcely audible. His arms encircled her in an instant. His cheek rested against hers, he felt her breath pass sighingly over it, and the spirit of Sophia had departed!

As soon as possible, after a long and dangerous illness, Wilmer went to Europe on sick certificate; his kinsman was dead, and had bequeathed to him a moderate competence, which enabled him to dedicate himself to the profound retirement he coveted. In a small house at Halle, once occupied by Madam Sternhof, lived years afterwards, a melancholy man, generally considered insane, at once shunning and shunned. The poor were well acquainted with him and his haunts, but, though he was suspected of an over great acquaintance with books, he was unknown both to the rich and the learned. His only attendant was the nurse of Sophia, whose fidelity, if he trusted her, was inviolable, for he was never betrayed. He was found dead one morning in a little arbour, the erection of which was well known to have been a favourite amusement to Sophia Sternhof, 'who had gone far away'. He was buried in the adjacent churchyard, in the corner shaded by the large and pale ash tree, where no headstone carried his name, his misfortunes, or his crimes.

Begum Sumroo's Escapade

A Muslim by birth, Begum Sumroo, née Zeb-un-Nissa, was an ambitious woman of extraordinary personal charm who ruled over the jagir of Sardhana, near Meerut, in the late eighteenth and early nineteenth century. She had risen from the lowly rank of a nautch girl to the high status of a Begum at a very young age by marrying a German soldier of fortune. This story of her life reveals her shrewdness and iron will in the face of heavy odds. After the death of her husband, she married again, at the age of 52, the French commander of her forces, but would not bear his family name following his suicide during their flight from Sardhana to seek British protection. She even allowed his body to suffer insults. Whether she was responsible for his death is not known but it cannot be denied that she had kept her second marriage a secret. A calculating woman, the Begum, when offered help by the authorities in her escape bid for a consideration, demanded in her turn a huge sum to give up command of her forces. Restored to her earlier position, she danced to the tune of the British, who found her to be a 'kind-hearted, benevolent' woman. By then she had adopted the European mode of social intercourse.

Begum Sumroo figures in quite a few contemporary journals of John Company officials and other European travellers. There are varying descriptions of the Begum's character and her doings. The version given in Rambles and Recollections of an Indian

Official *by Lt. Col W.H. Sleeman, on which this story is based, seems quite authentic. The author makes it a point to mention that 'I have nowhere indulged in fiction, either in the narrative, the recollections, or the conversations. What I relate on the testimony of others, I believe to be true, and what I relate upon my own you may rely upon as being so'.*

The Begum Sombre or Sumroo was by birth a Squadanee, or lineal descendant from Mahomed, the founder of the Mussulman faith; and she was united to Walter Reinhard when very young, by all the forms considered necessary by persons of her persuasion when married to men of another.

Walter Reinhard was a native of Saltsburg (sic). He enlisted as a private soldier in the French service, and came to India, where he entered the service of the East India Company, and rose to the rank of sergeant. Reinhard got the soubriquet of Sombre from his comrades while in the French service, from the sombre cast of his countenance and temper.

Sombre died at Agra, on the 4th May, 1778, and his remains were at first buried in his garden. They were afterwards removed to consecrated ground, in the Agra churchyard, by his widow, the Begum, who was baptized, at the age of forty, by a Roman Catholic priest, under the name of Joanna, on the 7th of May, 1781. On the death of her husband, she was requested to take command of the force by all the Europeans and natives that composed it, as the only possible mode of keeping them together, since the son from his first wife was known to be altogether unfit. She consented, and was regularly installed in the charge by the Emperor Shah Alam.

The command of the troops under the Begum, devolved successively upon Badurs, Evans, Dudrenee, who, after a

short time, all gave it up in disgust at the beastly habits of
the European subalterns, and the overbearing insolence to
which they and the want of regular pay gave rise among the
soldiers. At last the command devolved upon Monsieur Le
Vassoult, a French gentleman of birth, education, gentlemanly
deportment, and honourable feelings. The battalions had
been increased to six, with their due proportion of guns and
cavalry; part resided at Sirdhana, her capital, and part at
Delhi, in attendance upon the Emperor. A very extraordinary
man entered her service about the same time with Le Vassoult,
George Thomas, who, from a quarter-master on board a
ship, raised himself to a principality in northern India. Thomas
on one occasion raised his mistress in the esteem of the
Emperor and the people by breaking through the old rule of
central squares; gallantly leading on his troops, and rescuing
his majesty from a perilous situation in one of his battles
with a rebellious subject, Nujuf Coolee Khan, where the
Begum was present in her palankeen, and reaped all the
laurels, being from that day called 'the most beloved daughter
of the Emperor'. As his best chance of securing his ascendancy
against such a rival, Le Vassoult proposed marriage to the
Begum, and was accepted. She was married to Le Vassoult
by Father Gregorio, a Carmelite monk, in 1793, before Suleur
and Bernier, two French officers of great merit. George
Thomas left her service in consequence, in 1793, and set up
for himself; and was afterwards crushed by the united armies
of the Seikhs (sic) and Maharattas, commanded by European
officers, after he had been recognized as a general officer by
the Governor-General of India.

The Begum tried in vain to persuade her husband to
receive all the European officers of the corps at his table as
gentlemen, urging that not only their domestic peace, but

their safety among such a turbulent set, required that the character of these officers should be raised if possible, and their feelings conciliated. Nothing, he declared, should ever induce him to sit at table with men of such habits; and they at last determined, that no man should command them who would not condescend to do so. Their insolence, and that of the soldiers generally, became at last unbearable; and the Begum determined to go off with her husband, and seek an asylum in the honourable Company's territory with the little property she could command, of one hundred thousand rupees in money, and her jewels, amounting perhaps in value to one hundred thousand more. Le Vassoult did not understand English; but with the aid of a grammar and a dictionary he was able to communicate her wishes to Colonel M'Gowan, who commanded at that time, 1795, an advanced post of British army at Anoopshehur, on the Ganges. He proposed that the colonel should receive them in his cantonments, and assist them in their journey thence to Furuckabad, where they wished in future to reside, free from the cares and anxieties of such a charge. The colonel had some scruples, under the impression, that he might be censured for aiding in the flight of a public officer of the Emperor. He now addressed the Governor-General of India, Sir John Shore himself, (in) April, 1795, who requested Major Palmer, accredited agent with Scindeea (sic), who was then encamped near Delhi, and holding the seals of prime minister of the empire, to interpose his good offices in favour of the Begum and her husband. Scindeea demanded twelve lacks of rupees as the price of the privilege she solicited to retire; and the Begum, in her turn, demanded over and above the privilege of resigning the command into his hands, the sum of four lacks of rupees as the price of the arms and accoutrements which had been provided at her own cost and that of her late husband. It was at last settled, that she should resign the command, and set out secretly with her husband; and that Scindeea should confer the command of her troops upon one of his own officers, who would pay the son of Sombre two thousand rupees a month for life. Le Vassoult was to be received into British territories, treated as a prisoner of war upon his parole, and permitted to reside with his wife at the French settlement of Chandernagore.

The battalions on duty at Delhi got intimation of this agreement, made the son of Sombre declare himself their legitimate chief, and march at their head to seize the Begum and her husband. Le Vassoult heard of their approach, and urged the Begum to set out with him at midnight for Anoopshehur, declaring, that he would rather destroy himself than submit to the personal indignities which he knew would be heaped upon him by the infuriated ruffians who were coming to seize them. The Begum consented, declaring, that she would put an end to her life with her own hand should she be taken. She got into her palankeen with a dagger in her hand, and as he had seen her determined resolution and proud spirit before exerted on many trying occasions, he doubted not that she would do what she declared she would. He mounted his horse and rode by the side of her palankeen, with a pair of pistols in his holsters, and a good sword by his side. They had got on so far as Kabree, about three miles from Sirdhana, on the road to Merrut, when they found the battalions from Sirdhana, who had got intimation of the flight, gaining fast upon the palankeen. Le Vassoult asked the Begum, whether she remained firm on her resolve to die rather than submit to the indignities that threatened them. 'Yes,' replied she, showing him the dagger firmly grasped in her right hand. He drew a pistol from his holster without saying anything, but urged on the bearers. He could have easily galloped off and saved himself, but he would not quit his wife's side. At last, the soldiers came up close behind them. The female attendants of the Begum began to scream; and looking in, Le Vassoult saw the white cloth that covered the Begum's breast stained with blood. She had stabbed herself, but the dagger had struck against one of the bones of her chest, and she had not courage to repeat the blow. Her husband put his pistol to his temple, and fired. The ball passed through his head, and he fell dead on the ground. One of the soldiers who saw him, said that he sprung at least a foot off the saddle into the air as the shot struck him! His body was treated with every kind of insult by the European officers and their men; and the Begum was taken back into Sirdhana, kept under a gun for seven days, deprived of all kinds of food, save what she got by stealth from the female servants, and subjected to all manner of insolent language.

At last the officers were advised by George Thomas, who had instigated them to this violence out of pique against the Begum, for her preference of the Frenchman, to set aside their puppet, and reseat the Begum in the command, as the only chance of keeping the territory of Sirdhana. A counsel of war was held—the Begum was taken out from under the gun, and reseated upon her musnud. A paper was drawn up by about thirty European officers, of whom only one, Monsieur Saleur, could sign his own name, swearing, in the name of God and Jesus Christ, that they would henceforward obey her with all their hearts and souls, and recognise no other person whomsoever as commander. They all affixed their seals to this *covenant*; but some of them, to show their superior learning, put their initials, or what they used as such, for some of these *learned Thebans* knew only two or three letters of the alphabet, which they put down, though they happened not to be their real initials.

The body of poor Le Vassoult was brought back to camp, and there lay several days unburied, and exposed to all kinds of indignities. The supposition that this was the result of a plan formed by the Begum to get rid of Le Vassoult is believed to be unfounded. The Begum herself gave some colour of truth to the report, by retaining the name of her first husband, Sombre, to the last, and never publicly or formally declaring her marriage with Le Vassoult after his death. The troops in this mutiny pretended nothing more than a desire to vindicate the honour of their old commander Sombre, which had, they said, been compromised by the illicit intercourse between Le Vassoult and his widow. She had not dared to declare the marriage to them lest they should mutiny on that ground, and deprive her of the command; and for the same reason, she retained the name of Sombre after her restoration, and remained silent on the subject of her second marriage. The marriage was known only to a few European officers, Sir John Shore, Major Palmer, and the other gentlemen with whom Le Vassoult corresponded.

Among all who had opportunities of knowing her, she bore the character of a kind-hearted, benevolent, and good woman. She had uncommon sagacity, and a masculine resolution; and though a woman and of small stature, her *rooab* (dignity, or power of commanding personal respect) was greater than that of most persons of her days. From the time she put herself under the protection of the British government, in 1803, she by degrees adopted the European modes of social intercourse, appearing in public on an elephant, in a carriage, and occasionally on horseback with her hat and veil; and dining at table with gentlemen. She often entertained governors-general and commanders-in-chief, with all their retinues, and sat with them and their staff at table, and for some years past kept an open house for the society of Merrut; but in no situation did she lose sight of her dignity. She retained to the last the grateful affections of the thousands who were supported by her bounty, while she never ceased to inspire the most profound respect in the minds of those who every day approached her, and were on the most unreserved terms of intimacy.

Lord William Bentinck was an excellent judge of character; and the following letter will show how deeply his visit to that part of the country had impressed him with a sense of her extensive usefulness.

TO HER HIGHNESS THE BEGUM SUMROO

My esteemed Friend,—I cannot leave India without expressing the sincere esteem I entertain for your highness's character. The benevolence of disposition and extensive charity which have endeared you to thousands, have excited in my mind sentiments of the warmest admiration; and I trust that you may yet be preserved for many years, the solace of the orphan and widow, and the sure resource of your numerous dependants. To-morrow morning I embark for England; and my prayers and best wishes attend you, and all others who, like you, exert themselves for the benefit of the people of India.

I remain,

With much consideration,

Your sincere Friend,

M.W. BENTINCK. (signed)

Calcutta, March 17th, 1835

The Intrigues of a Nabob

Along with laying the foundations of the Empire in 1757, Clive heralded the age of the Nabob, a corruption of the Indian world 'nawab' (feudal landlord). The Nabobs were a class of wealthy British who had amassed fortunes, usually through dubious means. Clive himself was one of its shining lights. They hankered after power and prestige and used their positions to exploit whomsoever they could. Their morals and manners, fashions and foibles, were. ridiculed by their compatriots at home, who called them upstarts.

H.E. Busteed in his classic work, Echoes from Old Calcutta, *published in the beginning of the twentieth century, portrays a romantic picture of the social and political life of the British community in Calcutta. He recalls contemporary scandals and gossip about the famous and fashionable men and women during the days of Warren Hastings when Calcutta was known as one of the liveliest cities in the world.*

The author of a volume entitled as above was Mr Henry F. Thompson, who apparently held an appointment in the marine service of the East India Company. This gentleman, on returning to England from a voyage to the East, met in low society, and became enamoured of, a young person named Sarah Bonner, who, though at the time but sixteen years old, had already passed through some unfortunate vicissitudes which made the kindness and generosity that Thompson lavished upon her very acceptable. When the time came for the sailor's return to India, he discovered that he could not contemplate a long separation from one whom he had for some months protected; accordingly, as a means of avoiding this, and of providing an answer to inconvenient questions, he informed his friends that he had just married a wife, and then arranged that she and his own sister should be sent out together to Calcutta in a short time after him.

Of the sister no further mention is made.

When afterwards trying to account for his infatuation, Mr Thompson describes his enslaver as one 'whose charms were of the bewitching kind; they infused a soporiferous poison into the mind, benumbed and stuperfied the reasoning powers, and left her sole mistress of the head and heart of her lovers'.

Thompson returned to Bengal armed with letters to Governor Verelst, Mr Becher, and other influential officials; but all they could do for him was to get him appointed second officer of a ship then setting out on a voyage. When he got back to Calcutta from this voyage he found that the lady, who ever afterwards passed as 'Mrs Thompson' in Calcutta society, had arrived, and had been in Bengal since October 1769. Thompson immediately proceeded to make his nominal wife as comfortable as he could, and provided her with a house, which was 'genteely furnished, and soon honoured with the visits of persons of the first distinction of both sexes'. Amongst the distinguished visitors was Mr Richard Barwell, then holding an appointment in Calcutta. This benevolent man placed his suburban house at the disposal of the young couple, and shortly after obtained an appointment for Thompson, that of Deputy-Paymaster at

Berhampore, with 7000 rupees a year. To Berhampore, however, Mrs Thompson declined to go, avowing a preference for Calcutta, coupled with Mr Barwell's country house.

Thompson had not long taken up his appointment when certain changes in the official world at Calcutta got Barwell himself sent to Mootigeal, seven miles from Berhampore. His patron soon proposed that the Deputy-Paymaster should live with him. The latter agreed, and professed himself 'as happy as could be, wanting nothing but the society of the woman he held most dear'. Possibly it was with the object of breaking up an association, which it was foreseen would lead to a grave public scandal, that Thompson soon found himself suddenly and peremptorily recalled to Calcutta. In vain Barwell exerted his influence to get the order countermanded, but the government was inexorable, and Thompson went to the Presidency to wait for other employment. In the meantime he resumed his tenancy of Barwell's garden-house. The first shock which his feelings received on his arrival at Calcutta was from the coolness of the reception extended to him by his fair ensnarer; the next from his discovering after a little time that she was often surreptitiously receiving letters from Mootigeal, sent under cover to a Mr Cator, who was also occupying apartments in the garden-house. On contriving to see a little of this correspondence, the unwelcome fact became known to him that shortly after 'Mrs Thompson's arrival in Calcutta, while awaiting the sailor's return from the voyage previously mentioned, 'the sapper and miner was at work', as Sergeant Buzfuz puts it, Mr Barwell made her acquaintance, and had proceeded some lengths towards ingratiating himself. Any illusion he may have been under as to the disinterestedness of their patron's friendship must have been cruelly dispelled when he read that in Mr Barwell's opinion, he (Thompson) was 'a most uncouth semblance of humanity', 'a down-right man machine', whom the fair one was entreated to have no familiarities with of any kind. This was a point on which the absent admirer seemed to he nervously sensitive and exacting, for in one letter he expressed his apprehensions regarding the attentions of a Mr Robert Sanderson, who 'wishes to startle you or coax you to drop your connection with me, for the greater enjoyment his age and discretion are capable of affording you'. Coquetry must have been an effective weapon in the armoury of this Delilah, as the following passage was one which met Thompson's prying eye: 'You do my affections great wrong, and your own beauties great injustice; look in your glass, it will convince you you have charms capable of warming old age; can a young man be indifferent to them? I have exerted all my endeavours to effect the wish of my heart, and have drawn upon myself, in the attempt to keep your husband here, all that malevolence could invent to prejudice me in the estimation of my friends.' Unhappy, Mr Thompson was further doomed to find this somewhat rueful but candid sentiment: 'I love you, I wish you was with me and your husband at a distance.' The writer of the book leaves it to be inferred that he considered from passages in the discovered correspondence (such as this, 'No, my dear Madame, I will never ask any sacrifice to my peace that shall sink your name in the opinion of the world') it was not too late to save the woman, for whom he still retained affection, from taking any extreme step. He therefore said nothing of his discovery to Barwell, but told her that he would forgive everything if she would leave the country, and so withdraw herself from further temptation.

To this she had all but consented, when the tide of events

proved too strong for her. A sudden death in the upper ranks of the Civil Service gave promotion to Barwell, and again brought him to Calcutta. This accident opened up a prospect which the enterprising young lady was only too ready to make the most of. Very soon matters between her and Mr Barwell were in such train that she felt in a position to tell her first benefactor that 'his presence was eminently disagreeable', and to offer him, on the part of her new paramour, an annuity if he would betake himself out of India. She further stimulated his acceptance of her terms by threatening that, in case of refusal, she would make known her true position, and thus free herself from restraint. Even the ordinary capacity of Thompson realized what this alleged threat conveyed, viz. that if it came to a question of cold-blooded purchase much more might be squeezed out of Dives if he was allowed to remain under the impression that he was dealing with an injured husband instead of merely with a deserted lover. Thompson accordingly continued to dissemble; a bargain was struck, and a deed of trust was executed by Warren Hastings and Robert Sanderson, under which Barwell was to pay £5000 for the benefit of Sarah Thompson and her two children, and an annuity of £300 to Thompson, who was bound 'not to molest or trouble Mr Barwell on account of Mrs Thompson'. This occurred in March, 1772. It must not be forgotten that we have only got Thompson's side of this story.

To throw dust into the eys of society, it was next arranged that the ex-paymaster should go to China first, giving out that it was his intention to return to Calcutta. Eventually he made his way to Europe. He had not been there long when he received a letter from Mr Barwell telling him that 'it had become necessary to your own character, and the peace of your family, that you should make one more voyage to India, although you should immediately return to England with Mrs Thompson and the little ones'. In those days of slow voyages, much time must have elapsed before he again reached Calcutta in compliance with the request. He arrived but to find that the frail one had sailed for England in the *Anson* in September 1775. Public opinion, he says, had become too strong for Barwell; he had received official intimation that the scandal (intensified by the general impropriety of his companion) must no longer continue. Whether the very tolerant society of those days brought any pressure to bear on a member of Council may perhaps be open to question. It is just as likely that for Barwell the tempting fruit had turned to ashes. Indeed, we know from other sources that in this very year, 1775, he was proposing to himself to 'purge and live cleanly as a nobleman should'—to sow his wild oats and marry. At all events Thompson was informed that there was nothing for him to do but to go back again. This he agreed to do on condition of a fund being established for the sure payment of his annuity. No steps were taken towards this till he was on board ship, when Barwell provided him with a letter of instructions to his brother in London, and got him to 'sign a paper'.

When after a tedious voyage he produced the 'instructions' in London, he was told by Captain Barwell (also a sailor) that they gave him nothing whatever, and that the paper which he had signed before leaving India cancelled the deed formerly drawn. The latter part of the narrative is very obscure; the writer makes heavy drafts on the credulity of his readers regarding his own guileless and simple nature. The inference is perhaps legitimate that Barwell came to learn what the conspiring couple had concealed, and had availed himself of some proviso made in case of Thompson's failing to keep his side of the compact. In revenge Thompson told the story of his multitudinous sorrows for the edification of the British public. His book came out in 1780, the year in which his wronger left India. He gave it the alternative title of '*Or Bengal, the Fittest Soil for Lust*', and stuffed it full of letters said to have been written by Barwell during his brief madness to the charmer, who seems to have employed her 'soporiferous poison' to some purpose, as the victim's letters and poetry testify to the truth of the observation '*amare et sapere vix deo conceditur*'.

There is a coincidence or two suggested in these letters, and by some dates which come out in the narrative, that are worth recalling. In one Barwell says, 'I will write to Mr Imhoff about the picture', an allusion which goes to show that Imhoff was at this time in the bona fide practice of his profession. The Imhoffs and Mrs Thompson were old acquaintances, as they had been fellow-voyagers to India in the *Duke of Grafton* in 1769, which ship, it may be remembered, also carried, on the same voyage, Warren Hastings and his fortunes. It was possibly in consequence of this acquaintanceship that Hastings became one of the executors of the deed of trust aforesaid, in a week or two after his taking over the governorship of Bengal. He must have had misgivings as to complications of a delicate nature, arising out of the presence of Mrs Thompson in a community to which her fellow-passenger, Marian Imhoff, had been already translated from Madras. Mr Barwell's relations with Hastings' fellow-signatory Sanderson were of a curiously complicated nature. He began by being jealous of this gentleman, then made him trustee in his mistress's behalf, and concluded by marrying his daughter.

Reunion at Nagpore

The Empire provided an ideal setting for the heartbroken to heal their wounds. It was also perfect for those out to make a fortune the lack of which had prevented them from marrying their beloveds back home in England. Marriageable girls without the means to attract eligible bachelors flocked to India to hook husbands. Sometimes, high drama and suspense marked the course of events as in the following story in which a broken ring was instrumental in reuniting the lovers.

Women writers of the period have left lively accounts of the private lives of sahibs and memsahibs in the early days of the Raj. They were less concerned with tiger hunts and military expeditions and more with the British presence at the levels of family life and daily routine. One such writer was the author of this story, Mrs Major Clemons, whose interesting book, Manners and Customs of Society in India *(1841) is interspersed with a number of characteristic tales and anecdotes based on facts. In her introduction she clarifies that 'should the book meet the eye of any of the persons mentioned in its pages, I sincerely hope they will pardon my having used their names unauthorisedly', a liberty she occasionally deemed requisite as a more satisfactory proof of the authenticity of many of the scenes she depicted; 'with this apology I throw myself upon their generosity'.*

Henry Harling was the younger branch of a noble family; his father died when he was about fourteen years old, and his mother, the honourable Mrs Harling, was a woman of haughty, imperious disposition, who had but a small jointure to support her hereditary pride, while her mind had dwelt long and ardently on attaining a suitable match for her son, who had no fortune to step into when he came of age, nor were his expectations of future title and estates more cheering; as there were four between him and the possession of such distinctions, for his uncle, Lord Molestock, had three sons, youths of nearly the same age as himself, all of good constitutions and likely to live and marry, thereby rendering the removes from the title still more distant.

Henry Harling cared little for money; he was of a bold, generous disposition, and the small sum allowed him by his mother for his private expenses while at college was amply sufficient.

Mrs Harling, while in the country, found, with the most rigid economy, that she might with more éclat be seen amongst the fashionables in London, during the winter season.

Her country residence was in Devonshire; it was a lovely cottage near the sea. There were a few families that she visited in the neighbourhood, amongst whom was the Rev. Mr Grey, his wife and daughter. Miss Grey was highly accomplished; she had had every advantage of good and solid education, which her father, from her very infancy, had given her; added to which, masters for the more showy accomplishments had been procured for her, and her naturally quick intellect had aided her in the acquirement of every kind of useful knowledge. Mr Grey could give her no fortune; therefore he used to say, 'Poor Emily, when I am gone, and leave you in a bleak world alone, your education will be an income to you.' She was very lovely; her dark blue eyes sparkled with intelligence; her hair waved in natural ringlets over her fair brow; the rosy hue of health was on her cheek, and the smile of good temper played round her small mouth; she was only seventeen, and the wildness of childish playfulness had not yet passed away. Mrs Harling much admired the lovely Emily, for she was useful to her; her harp and voice amused her; her society in a ramble broke the tediousness of green fields and lanes, and her conversation dispelled ennui, while her peculiar liveliness and naivete became almost essential to her comfort; so that when Mrs Harling was at Rose Cottage, Emily was constantly there.

There was also another family whom she frequently visited, a Mr Thompson. He had been a Liverpool merchant, and had accumulated an immense fortune; his only daughter, about twenty-three years old, unfortunately was deformed, and remarkably plain. She had lost her mother when very young, and being the heiress of 200,000 pounds, she had been indulged by all; her governess was not allowed to insist upon her learning anything, as her health was delicate; consequently she was neither well educated nor accomplished. Still she was naturally good-tempered, kind, and obliging. Her father had only removed into Devonshire for the sake of her health, and they had been settled about four years at the castle, in the immediate neighbourhood of Mrs Harling. Laura Thompson was the person whom Mrs Harling had fixed on in her own mind as a suitable wife for her son, and she had endeavoured, for the last two years, in every possible way, to bring about a marriage between them. During the two months that Henry spent in Devonshire every year, she invited Laura to stay with her, thinking that by accustoming him to her constantly, he might be more easily led into her views, and not think so much of her plainness. She had also taken great care to prevent him being too much with the lovely Emily; she could not, indeed, altogether keep her out of his sight, but she had always said to her, 'When my son's at home, I like to be much alone with him, as it is for such a short time in the year; so dear, you must not think me neglectful of you if I seldom see you.' All her precautions, however, were vain; the interesting and beautiful Emily stole into Henry's heart, and took a firm and lasting hold of his affections; nor was the image less cherished in the bosom of Emily herself.

It was during his last college term that Mrs Harling proposed to him the eligible match that Miss Thompson would be to him. Now he was to leave college, it was necessary he should settle in life by marriage, or bend his mind to some profession. He well knew she had no fortune to give him, and at her death he would be quite destitute, and dependent on the bountry of his uncle, Lord Molestock. She went on to say that she had mentioned her wishes to Mr Thompson, who was perfectly willing to bestow his rich heiress on him, provided the young lady herself made no objection; and she was quite certain of the affections of the lady—indeed she had hinted to her how much she wished her to be her daughter-in-law, and Laura had only blushed, hung her head, and exclaimed that Henry was a charming young man. Henry opened to his mother the state of his heart, and the decided rejection of all her matrimonial plans for him. 'What, dear mother,' said he, 'would you wed me to ignorance and deformity? Would you blast your son's hope of happiness, for the sake of a few thousand pounds? You have been ever to me a kind friend; you will not surely now insist upon a marriage that will not fail to make me for ever wretched: oh! no, my mother, my heart and warmest love is given to Emily; none other shall supplant her image in my breat; I will be true to her for ever!'

'Henry, cease!' cried Mrs Harling; 'my mind is made up: the money you get by acceding to my proposal, will amply purchase your happiness. Henry, I have long lived in retirement; what were the motives of that seclusion? To be enabled to give you an education suitable to your birth, and to your future career. I have scrimped myself, lived upon a pittance, to give you a distinguished footing in the world; it is now my turn to reap the advantages of my self-denial: you must now place your mother in society again. Emily Grey shall never, with my consent, be your wife: think well, therefore, before you decide. I give you one week; in the meantime, I insist upon your company being devoted to Laura.' On the following day Henry met Emily and told her the conversation he had had with his mother; he then went on: 'I know my mother too well to believe that she will ever alter her present determination; but never, dear Emily, will I be induced to make Laura Thompson my wife.'

'Oh Henry, it will break my heart to part from you! but never will I be in the way of your interests. No, dear Henry, marry Laura, and forget the humble Emily; besides 'tis your duty; you owe it to your mother for all her former fond care of you.'

'My dearest,' said he, at length, 'I owe my mother duty and affection; but not to the extent of debasing myself. I have made up my mind to leave this place at the end of the week, if I cannot, after every solicitation and argument, bring my mother to receive you as her daughter, even at some distant period; and should I gain her consent thus far, would you, my dearest Emily, consent to a private marriage, as it would lessen the dreadful anxiety of absence?'

'Henry, no argument can induce me to do what I consider wrong: my beloved father and mother taught me that concealment of any kind is wrong; how much more so in such a momentous affair as this. You must doubt my love for you, Henry; but I swear to you never to love another, never to be persuaded to accept another as a husband: will that satisfy you, love? Claim me years hence, when no impediment may exist to our union, and I am yours for ever.'

'My own darling Emily, I believe firmly in your truth, and will rest satisfied, however distant I am from you. Here, let me place this ring on your finger, and now, in the face of Heaven, do I call you my wife, and never will I wed another.' Thus they parted.

The week expired. Henry Harling again tried to gain his mother's consent to his wishes, or even to give up her plans for his interest; but all he could say was useless, and they parted with high words on both sides.

On the following morning, when Mrs Harling came down to breakfast, she found a note on the table from her son, saying that he had left for London, and it was quite uncertain when he should return. Day after day went on, and week after week passed away, and still she heard nothing of him; she knew not what to think; she did not like to write to Lord Molestock about him, as she was unwilling to show how little her son cared for the authority of his mother. She called at the parsonage, but could gain no information. Emily looked pale and anxious, but never even asked after her son, this showed that she knew something. Another month passed on, and still he neither came nor wrote. At length she determined to go to London: previously, however, she resolved to question Emily; for her mind was becoming too uneasy to admit of any more scruples. Her kindness to Emily had never abated; she loved her as much as an interested woman could love any who was not subservient to her own wishes. She saw her superiority over Laura, and her only objection to the former was her want of fortune. Two hundred thousand pounds was weighed in the balance, and Emily was found wanting.

On Mrs Harling's visit to the Greys, she at once put the question: 'My dear Emily,' said she, 'have you heard of my son since he has left this place?' Emily scarcely knew what to answer: but she had always been taught to be ingenuous, so with a deep blush she replied that she had heard once, but only once, from Mr Harling during his long absence, and she showed her the letter which ran thus:

My dearest Emily will not think I have forgotten her by being thus long in writing; my mind has been much harassed; but now that my plans are settled, I feel a relief—a comparative happiness, which, however, will never be completed till I clasp my adored Emily to my breast as my wife; never will I cease to love you. Now, Emily, I beg of you never for a moment to think my affections are changed, should it even be months, long months before you hear from me again; nor must you think me unkind, if you are not informed where I am. I firmly believe in your truth; do you trust in mine. Be kind to my mother, who I know loves me, though she has shown it rather ungenerously in wishing to force my inclinations, and in being deaf to my earnest entreaties. Farewell, dearest, beloved Emily, the day will come when, I trust, we shall be happy in each other. Ever your devotedly attached,

Henry Harling

'And can you form no idea,' said Mrs Harling, 'from any conversation you may have had previously, where he has gone? and what he intends to do?'

'None, madam, whatever.'

Mrs Harling soon after quitted the house, and in a day or two left Devonshire for London. On her arrival there, she found that Henry had never called at his uncle's, nor could she gain any intelligence of him whatever.

Two years passed away in vain conjectures. The mother deeply deplored the loss of her son, and at times thought that could she bring him back again she would even sanction his marriage with Emily. These two years were eventful ones to that poor girl.

A little more than a year after Harling left Devonshire, Mr Grey died suddenly of apoplexy; this was a dreadful blow to Mrs Grey and her daughter; added to the overwhelming sorrow for his loss, was the poverty in which they were left. The widow had a small pension, but very inadequate to their maintenance. With the help of Mr Thompson Emily secured the position of a governess with Mr and Mrs Davenport who were returning to Madras with their three daughters.

They sojourned at Madras only for a short time after their arrival in India, as Mr Davenport was made collector, and ordered to be stationed at Nagpore. They were both much pleased with Emily. Her retiring modesty, and her extreme beauty created the admiration of every one. Numerous were the visitors at Mrs Davenport's house to see the pretty governess, and sad was the disappointment when she did not make her appearance; for it was only at breakfast and dinner, or a little time in the evening that she could be seen.

Mrs Davenport had the good sense to treat her daughter's governess as a lady, not as a kind of upper servant, which is too frequently the case in England; but she was made in every respect equal to herself, and by this means the young ladies felt a pleasure in receiving instructions from her, and they themselves looked up to her, and loved her as a real friend.

They had been stationed at Nagpore about six months, and during that time Emily had received two most eligible offers of marriage; one of them from Colonel Townsend of the Infantry, the other from Colonel Windham of the Artillery; both of which she declined accepting, though she was much urged by Mrs and Mr Davenport to accept one of them. She frankly told Mrs Davenport that her hand and affections were engaged to a gentleman in England, though she thought it probable that circumstances would interfere to prevent their ever being united. To Colonel Windham she also made known her engagement to Harling, as she saw that he was determined to persevere in his addresses to her.

It was about this time that an accident happened to the ring that Henry had given her, which she had constantly worn since the night he had placed it on her finger. It was a large, handsome ruby, set around with small brilliants, and peculiar in its setting and workmanship; it had always been a little too large for her, and she supposed, that in walking one evening in the verandah, she must have pulled it off with her glove; for, on going to her room at night, she found her cherished gift of love gone. A search was immediately made for it, and it was found broken in two pieces. It had most probably received the injury from its having been trodden on. Emily felt exceedingly sorry that this accident should have happened to her ring, and begged Mrs Davenport's butler to get it immediately repaired for her; but she said that it must be taken to the best workman in the place, as she much valued the ring.

The butler replied that there was a European in the Artillery who could work in this way, and had a good deal of business; he was one of the sergeants, and he would therefore take it to him. The butler accordingly went with the ring, and found the sergeant at home, and at work, mending a necklace. Two of the artillery-men were talking to him. On the butler's presenting the ring for the inspection of the sergeant, one of the men turned round, and said, 'Let me look at the ring, will you? I think I have seen it before.'

'Certainly, replied the sergeant, 'it is a very handsome ruby.'

The artillery-man, whose name was Field, became much agitated. 'Pray,' said he to the butler, 'whose servant are you? Speak, sir.'

'Mrs Davenport's,' replied the man 'and my young mistress gave me this ring to get mended, and she told me I was to take it to the best workman, and she had a great value for it.'

'Your young mistress,' said Field, 'how long has she been in this country?'

'Why, I believe about a year,' replied the butler: 'they hired me at Madras, just after they arrived from England.'

'You are ill, Field,' said the sergeant: 'sit down, man what has all this to do with you?'

'Oh, nothing,' replied Field; 'it was only a little curiosity—that's all. Good afternoon, sergeant;' and Field left the house.

The next day Field came again to the sergeant's house, and asked him if the ring were done, and if he would oblige him by allowing him to take it back to Mrs Davenport; he would pledge himself, he said, for its safe delivery.

The sergeant consented, and Field bent his steps to the collector's residence. On his arrival there, he begged one of the peons in waiting to tell Mrs Davenport that he had brought home the ring, which had been sent to be mended, and if she were not engaged, he would wish to see herself, and deliver it into her own hands. Field stood in the centre of the room, pale and motionless, with his eyes fixed on the opposite door, through which the peon had disappeared. At length the door opened, and Mrs Davenport entered. The statue-like appearance of Field startled her for a moment. 'Did you wish to see me?' she gently said.

'Are you Mrs Davenport?' said he, almost breathless, without answering her question, and with his hands extended towards her.

'Yes,' replied that lady.

'Thank God,' said Field, as he clasped his hands, and turned to leave the room; but suddenly stopping, he again advanced towards Mrs Davenport, who was still standing near the door by which she had entered the room, as if to be ready to make her escape, should it be necessary. 'I beg your pardon, Madam,' said Field, 'but my mind has been wrought up almost to madness, believing you to be another person, and seeing you has quite overpowered me. This ring, Madam, is so like one belonging to a dear friend of mine in England, that I have been deceived in imagining it the same. I trust I may be forgiven for having probably, by my unguarded manner, caused you some alarm.' He bowed low, smiled, and left the room.

Mrs Davenport stood, for a few moments, in astonishment at this address, 'Strange!' thought she—'a common soldier too, and so gentlemanly, so much elegance in his manners.' He had placed the ring in her hand: she looked at it. 'It certainly is of curious workmanship,' mused she, 'few, I should think, would exactly resemble it.' She left the room, and joined the young ladies in their morning study.

'Miss Grey,' said she, 'the man has brought back your ring; it is very curiously set. May I ask where you had it from? Did it belong to your poor father, my dear?'

'No, Madam,' replied Emily, with her natural frankness; 'it was given to me as a keepsake by the nephew of Lord Molestock,' and she blushed a deep scarlet as she again placed it on her finger. 'Then, indeed,' exclaimed Mrs Davenport, 'the man must have been mistaken, or else he was mad; for he fancied me to be some other person, and thought that he knew the ring. His manner really frightened me at first; but I will not interrupt your studies, my dears:— go on, Fanny, with your music.' She now left the room.

When the duties of the morning were over, and Emily was seated in her dressing-room, she could not help thinking on what Mrs Davenport had said regarding the man who had brought the ring; and a wild fancy crept over her mind, 'it is certainly very odd', she kept repeating to herself. At length she sent for the butler, and on his appearance, she asked him to whom he had taken her ring to be mended, and what was his name; also how old he was, and what sort of a looking person.

'He is a sergeant, ma'am, belonging to the Artillery,' said the butler: 'he is rather a short and fat man, and I should think about fifty years old; he has a wife and several children, ma'am, and she takes in needle-work for ladies, ma'am.'

Emily smiled as the butler concluded, to think how her air-built castles had vanished. 'I thank you,' said she, 'here are three rupees: be so kind as to pay the man. I am very well pleased with the manner in which he has mended the ring.'

Emily had now been about two years in India. The eldest Miss Davenport was married; and the second, though only sixteen years old, was engaged to a gentleman, and the marriage was shortly to take place; so that she had only to superintend the education of the youngest. Mrs Davenport had become so much attached to Emily, that she dreaded the probability of her leaving her. She had also insisted upon her being much in company of late, in the hope that she would ultimately settle in India by an advantageous marriage. She considered that a girlish attachment, where there was no hope to feed upon, as she supposed to be the case with Emily, would naturally give place, in time, to one of the many offers of marriage she had had while residing with her.

One morning, while they were all at breakfast, Colonel Windham, the Commandant of the Artillery, came in, and after a little conversation mentioned that he had received a curious letter from the Commander-in-Chief, ordering him to parade his men, as it was ascertained, beyond a doubt, that Lord Molestock was a private in the corps.

'Indeed,' said Emily, 'that is very strange; old Lord Molestock must be dead then, and his eldest son—for he had three—must have come to India as a private soldier. What could have induced him to leave his country in this manner, for they have all handsome fortunes, quite independent of the old Lord.'—'It is an odd circumstance,' continued the Colonel, 'I have an immense sealed packet from Government, directed to him, besides my private orders regarding the affair; it will be rather an interesting sight. Suppose you all come, ladies; I have ordered parade at half-past five this evening.'

'Indeed, I should ' like to see it very much,' replied Mrs Davenport. 'What say you, Miss Grey?—it is seldom that I can get you to accompany me to see sights; but as you know something of the family,' glancing slily at the ring on Emily's finger, 'you will feel interested in the discovery of this noble gentleman in the ranks.'

'It will afford me much pleasure,' said Emily.

'Well, then, agreed,' cried Mrs Davenport: 'we shall be very punctual to the hour Colonel.'

Emily felt all the day exceedingly anxious, she knew not why; for she had never seen any of Mr Harling's family, and consequently could not know the person of Lord Molestock. However, she could settle to none of her usual avocations, and was ready to enter the barouche long before the appointed time. At a little after five o'clock the four ladies drove from the door, accompanied by Mr Davenport on horseback.

The men were drawn up to form three sides of a square as closely as possible; the officers in the centre; and the two or three carriages that were there were arranged on the other side. The Colonel was the only person who was mounted.

'Soldiers, attention!' said he. 'This paper I have today received from Government. It is known deeply to concern one man amongst the eight hundred now present; I therefore command you to listen most attentively.' He read: 'To Colonel Windham, commanding the Artillery: Sir, I am directed to inform you that, owing to a melancholy accident caused by the upsetting of a boat off the coast of Cornwall, Lord Molestock and his three sons have lost their lives. The title and estates, besides all the personal property, now devolves upon his nephew, Henry Harling, son of the late General Harling, and youngest brother of the late Lord Molestock. This gentleman has been traced through the India House and elsewhere, and we find that, nearly four years ago, he entered the Company's Artillery, on the Madras establishment, as a private soldier. To further identify the said Henry Harling, now Lord Molestock; he is five feet ten inches in height, dark hair and whiskers, dark blue eyes with black lashes, a long Grecian nose, rather florid complexion, and good teeth. You are further directed, on the discovery of the above person, to present him with the enclosed packet. But should no such person be found in your Artillery, you are directed to communicate the same to the right honourable the Governor at Madras, that further search may be made in other European regiments, as the said Henry Harling may have exchanged; and in the event of any person answering to the above description having died within the last six months, you are directed forthwith to communicate the same to the right honourable the Governor.—I have the honour to be, your obedient servant, J.DASHWOOD, Major, Secretary to the Right Hon. the Governor.'

Every word of this paper was distinctly heard by all who were present. Emily sat motionless with half-suspended breath to catch every sound. She had thrown off her veil in her anxiety to hear every word. When the letter was concluded, she started up in the carriage and leant over the side of it, endeavouring more distinctly to see each man as he stood erect in the lines. At length the front rank of the near company broke a little, in the centre, a slight bustle was seen, and a man from the second rank walked a few paces in front; he then raised his cap from his head, and facing the Colonel, said 'I am Henry Harling; I am now Lord Molestock.'

Emily had seen the movement in the lines; she had seen the man advance, and watched with the utmost intensity the lifting of the military cap from his head and when she saw the well-known face, she forgot all around her in the surprise and agitation of the moment and leaped from the seat of the carriage to the ground; she ran a pace or two, and then fainted.

Colonel Windham was not far from the carriage, and saw her leap down and fall. He still loved Emily, though he had long since ceased to hope that she could return it, from her candour towards him: he sprang from his horse and exclaimed, 'Miss Grey is killed.'

'Miss Grey!' cried Harling, as he dashed his hat to the ground, and ran to the carriage, 'My own Emily! Yes it is!' and he pushed past the Colonel, and supported Emily in his arms—'Look up, dearest, look up, now that I can claim you as my own!'

Emily opened her eyes. 'Henry!' she cried, 'it is indeed you!' and she again relapsed into insensibility. She was immediately placed in the carriage.

Mrs Davenport looked at Harling, and recognized the man who brought the ring to her house, 'Ah!' said she to him with a smile and a tear, 'I can now understand the mystery of the ring! Come to my house by and bye; now, you cannot follow us.'

'No,' replied the Colonel, 'though now Lord Molestock, you are still for the present my soldier, and under my command; so follow me to my house. I cannot for a moment doubt your identity; Miss Grey has fully established that fact.'

Lord Molestock, as we must now call him, bowed. The parade was dismissed, and the Colonel, having sent home his horse, walked with Henry to his bungalow, where he delivered to him the packet addressed to him. It contained letters of credit to a large amount, also an affectionate letter from his mother, one from his, lawyer, and his discharge from the Company's service. Letters were dispatched to Government by that night's post from himself, as well as from the Colonel; a packet was also partly made up for England, and when all this business was done, the good Colonel shook hands with him, and congratulated him most sincerely, not only for his acquisition of fortune, but upon the prospect of a happy union with his beloved Emily,—'and I can assure you,' continued he, 'that I have done all I can to possess the sweet girl for a wife, and so have many others; however, she has been true to you, though surrounded by a host of admirers.'

We may well imagine the delight which Emily felt as she prepared to meet her beloved Henry after such a long absence, and all the circumstances attending on it. As for Mrs Davenport, she was in an ecstasy, kissed her favourite a hundred times, put off the dinner till eight o'clock, kept looking at her watch, and running from Emily to Mr Davenport, thinking he would never come, and that the good old Colonel was a prosy creature to keep him, and fixed in her own mind all about the wedding, and that her Fanny must be married on the same day.

As soon as Lord Molestock had finished his business with the Colonel, he proceeded directly to Mr Davenport's, and was shown into the very room where but a few months before, he had entered a miserable man, thinking that in Mrs Davenport he should behold his beloved Emily.

A happy half-hour of explanation was passed between the lovers; and as Lord Molestock was obliged to return to England immediately, Emily consented to become his wife the following week, and sail with him. Never perhaps did week pass away in greater happiness and bustle of preparations. Emily deeply regretted the parting with her kind friends, and many tears did she shed on the bosom of Mrs Davenport, who had indeed been to her a mother in a foreign land. Her beloved pupils also wept bitterly at the thought of her departure.

The morning of the marriage arrived; the ceremony took place at nine o'clock, and the Artillery men had the pleasure of firing a salute in honour of their late mess-mate, as he returned to breakfast at Mr Davenport's.

Before Lord Molestock left Nagpore, he distributed money and suitable presents to every man in the company, with whom he had passed nearly four years, nor was the sergeant and his family forgotten. Lord Molestock, as the private Field, had been much beloved by all in the regiment. Many of them considered he was of higher rank than he pretended to: he was always kind to them, though he mixed little in their amusements, and his uniform steadiness and respectful conduct had gained him the goodwill of all the officers.

'Harling's story' soon reached Hyderabad, and when Lord and Lady Molestock came within a few miles of that city on their route to Madras, the British Resident sent out his coach-and-four with a guard of honour to conduct them in. The Artillery fired a salute as they entered the cantonment.

After a quick and prosperous passage they arrived in England. Emily was soon clasped in her mother's arms, and Mrs Harling welcomed them both with delight, and strained them to her breast. Her ambition was fully gratified; her beloved son was a Peer, and had an ample estate. She now felt proud in her son's choice of a wife, and was well satisfied that he had not been persuaded to marry the plain, but amiable Miss Thompson, who still resided in Devonshire, unmarried and in very bad health.

An Invisible Attraction

English young men coming to India to join the East India Company as cadets or writers were called 'griffins', the newcomers. The ordinary period of griffinhood was one year, at the end of which they were expected to acquire sufficient familiarity with the language, customs and manners of the country, and also learn about the lifestyle of the British community in India. There is an absorbing account in Captain Bellew's Memoirs of a Griffin *(1843) of a gallant young man, Frank Gernon, who with his influential family contacts and an old India connection through his uncle secured a cadetship with the John Company. Smitten by love from his early boyhood days, he proved his prowess in the affairs of the heart. He won over, so he thought, the love of a charming girl in Madras, but his dream was nipped in the bud through no fault of his. However, in Calcutta at the age of eighteen he had his heart's fulfilment in the company of a widow four years senior to him: What did a little disparity matter, he told himself!*

Capt. Bellew's two-volume Memoirs of a Griffin, *from which this story is taken, had first appeared in a somewhat different form in* The Asiatic Journal. *The author says he has 'blended fact and fiction though always endeavouring to keep the vrai-semblable in view', adding that 'my wish has been to amuse and where I could to instruct and improve'.*

Love, that passion productive of so many pains and pleasure to mortals, the most easily, perhaps, awakened, and the most difficult to control, begins full early with some of us (idiosyncratically susceptible) to manifest its disturbing effects: the little volcano of the heart (to speak figuratively) throws out its transient and flickering flames long anterior to a grand eruption. Lord Byron's history exhibits a great and touching example of this; his early but unrequited attachment to the beautiful Miss Chaworth served undoubtedly, in after-life, to tinge his character with that sombre cast which has imparted itself to the splendid creations of his immortal genius. Like him (if I may dare include myself in the same category), when but nine or ten summers had passed over my head, I too had my 'lady love', who, albeit no Mary Chaworth, was nevertheless a very pretty little blue-eyed girl, the daughter of our village doctor. I think I now behold her, in the eye of my remembrance, with her white muslin frock, long pink sash, and necklace of coral beads, her flaxen curls flying wildly in the breeze, or sporting in all conceivable lines of beauty over her alabaster neck and forehead. Full joyous was I when an invitation came for Master Frank Gernon and his brother Tom to drink tea at Dr Anodyne's. How motherly and kind was good Mrs Anodyne on these occasions! How truly liberal of her pound-cake and syllabub!

Pretty Louisa! my first love, long since perhaps the mother of a tribe of little rustics; or sleeping, perchance, soundly in your own village churchyard! Like a fairy vision, you sometimes visit me in my dreams, or, when quitting for a season the stem, hard realities which environ my manhood, I lose myself in the sweet remembrances of boyhood's days! Well, this was my first grand love affair; now for my next, I fell over head and ears in love with lovely Olivia whom I met at Mr Hearty's house in Madras, where I had stayed as a guest during the ship's stopover there.

The party at Mr Hearty's, or some of them, rode out every evening in the carriage, and I generally, like a gallant griffin, took up a position by the steps, for the purpose of handing them in—that is, the female portion. The precise amount of pressure which a young lady of sixteen (not stone, but years, be pleased to understand, for it makes a material difference) must impart to a young gentleman's hand, when he tenders his services on occasions of this nature, in order to be in love with him, is a very nice and curious question in 'Amorics' (I take credit for the invention of that scientific term). In estimating it, however, so many things may affect the accuracy of a judgement, that it is perhaps undesirable to rely on deductions therefrom, either one way or the other, as a secure basis for ulterior proceedings. Touching the case of the charming Olivia and myself, though there was certainly evidence of the high-pressure system, I might long have felt at a loss to decide on the real state of her feelings, had not my hand on these occasions been accepted with a tell-tale blush, and a sweet and encouraging smile, that spoke volumes. Let me not be accused of vanity, if I say, then, that the evidence of my having made an impression on the young and susceptible heart of Olivia Jenkins was too decided to be mistaken. I felt that I was a favourite, and I burned with all the ardour of a griffin to declare that the 'sentiment si doux' was reciprocal. The wished for occasion was not long in presenting itself.

One evening, Olivia and some of the party remained at home, the carriage being fully occupied without them. Off drove Mr and Mrs Hearty, and a whole posse of friends and visitors, to take their usual round by Chepauk and the Fort, kissing hands to Olivia and one or two others, who stood on the terrace to see them depart. They were no sooner gone than I proceeded to enjoy my accustomed saunter in the coconut grove, at the back of the house. There was a delicious tranquillity in the hour which produced a soothing effect on my feelings. The sun had just dipped his broad orb in the ocean, and his parting beams suffused with a ruddy warmth the truly Oriental scene around. Flocks of paroquets, screaming with delight, were wheeling homewards their rapid flight; the creak of the well-wheel, an Indian rural sound, came wafted from distant fields, and the ring-doves were uttering their plaintive cooings from amidst the shady bowers of the neighbouring garden—

The air, a chartered libertine, was still.

I walked and mused, gazing around on the animated scenes of nature, which always delight me, when suddenly one of the most charming of all her works, a beautiful girl, appeared before me. It was Olivia, who met me (undesignedly of course) at a turn of the avenue. She appeared absorbed in a book, which, on hearing my steps, she suddenly closed and with a blush, which caused the eloquent blood to mount responsive in my cheeks, she exclaimed, 'Oh, Mr Gernon, is this you? Your servant, Sir! (courtesying half-coquettishly); who would have expected to meet you here all alone, and so solemnly musing?'

'Is there anything more extraordinary in it, Miss Olivia,' said I, 'than to find you also alone, and enjoying your intellectual repast, "under the shade of melancholy boughs?" The Chinese, I believe, think that human hearts are united from birth by unseen silken cords, which, contracting slowly but surely, bring them together at last. What think you,

Olivia?' I continued (we grow familiar generally on the eve of a declaration), 'may not some such invisible means of attraction have brought us together at this moment?'

Olivia looked down, her pretty little foot being busily engaged in investigating the character of a pebble, or something of the sort, that lay on the walk, and indistinctly replied, that she had really never much considered such weighty and mysterious subjects, but that it might be even so. Encouraged by this reply, yet trembling at the thought of my own audacity (bullets whizzing past me since have not produced half the trepidation), I placed myself near her, and gently taking the little, soft, white hand which listlessly, but invitingly, hung by her side, I said (I was sorely puzzled what to say),

'I-I-was delighted, dear Olivia, to find you a visitor here on my arrival the other day.'

'Were you, Mr Gernon,' said the lively girl, turning upon me her soft blue eyes, in a manner which brought on a fresh attack of *delirium tremens*; "delighted" is a strong term, but Mr Gernon, I know, is rather fond of such, little heeding their full import.'

'Strong!' I replied, instantly falling into heroics; 'it but feebly expresses the pleasure I feel on seeing you. Oh, dearest Olivia,' I continued, all the barriers of reserve giving way at once before the high tide of my feelings, 'it is in vain longer to dissemble' (here I gently passed my other unoccupied arm round her slender waist); 'I love you with the fondest affection. Deign to say that I possess an interest in your heart.'

A slight and almost imperceptible increase of pressure from the little hand locked in mine, and a timid look from the generally lively but now subdued and abashed girl, was the silent but expressive answer I received. It was enough, for a griff, at least. I drew her closer to my side—she slowly averted her head; mine followed its movement. The vertebral column had reached its rotatory limit—so that there was a sort of surrender at discretion and I imprinted a long and fervent kiss on the soft and downy cheek of Olivia. Oh, blissful climax of a thousand sweet emotions; too exquisite to endure too precious for fate to accord more than once in an existence—the first innocent kiss of requited affection—how can I ever forget ye?

> Let raptured fancy on that moment dwell,
> When my fond vows in trembling accents fell;
> When love acknowledged woke the trembling sigh,
> Swelled my fond breast and filled the melting eye.

Yes, surely, 'love is heaven, and heaven is love', as has been said and sung any time for the last three thousand years; and Mahomed shewed himself deeply read in the human heart when he made the chief delight of his paradise to consist in it; not, I suspect, as is generally imagined, the passion in its purely gross acceptation, but that elevating and refining sentiment which beautifully attunes all our noblest emotions; which, when it swells the heart, causes it to overflow, like a manting fountain, to refresh and fertilize all around. No, I shall never forget the thrill of delight with which I committed that daring act of petty larceny.

'Yes,' I continued, 'dearest Olivia, I have long loved you. I loved you from the first, and would fain indulge a faint hope' (this was hypocritical, for I was quite sure of it) 'that I am not wholly indifferent to you.'

The deepest blush overspread Olivia's neck and face; she was summoning all her maidenly resolution for an avowal: 'Dear Mr Gernon,' she said, 'believe me—'

'Stop him! stop him, Gernon,' roared a stentorian voice at this moment; 'cut the deevil off fra' the tree!'

It was that confounded Patagonian Scotch cadet, in full cry after a squirrel, which, poor little creature, in an agony of fear, was making for a tree near to which we stood. 'As you were', never brought a recruit quicker into his prior position than did this unseasonable interruption restore me to mine. Olivia hastily resumed her studies and her walk, whilst I, to prevent suspicion, and consequent banter, joined in the chevy to intercept the squirrel, secretly anathematizing Sandy McGrigor, whom I wished, with all my heart, in the bowels of Ben Lomond.

Reader, you may be curious to know whether Olivia Jenkins became in due time Mrs Gernon. Ah, no! Ours was one of those juvenile passions destined to be nipped in the bud; one of those painted baubles, swelled by the breath of young desire, which float for a brief space on the summer breeze, then burst and disappear: or a perennial plant, whose beautiful maturity passes rapidly to decay.

Our destinies pointed different ways. Too much calculation was fatal to her happiness; too little has been, perhaps, as detrimental to mine. Years on years rolled on, chequered by many strange vicissitudes, when, in other scenes and under widely different circumstances, we met again: the flush of youth had long departed from her cheeks, the once laughing eyes were brilliant no more—and

> The widow's sombre cap concealed
> Her once luxuriant hair.

'Do you remember,' said I, adverting to old times, 'our meeting in the coconut grove at Madras?'

'Ah!' she replied, with a sigh, 'I do indeed; but say no

more of it; a recurrence to the sun-shiny days of my youth always makes me sad: let us speak of something else—the recent, the present, the future.'

The next girl to come in my life was the young widow Mrs Cordalia Delaval, the daughter of General Capsicum to whom I carried a letter of introduction. She had got on board at Madras and travelled with us to Calcutta. On arriving at the General's house in Calcutta, I was shewn upstairs into the drawing-room, which commanded a pleasant view of the Hoogly. I was standing gazing on the prospect, admiring the boats under sail gliding from side to side, when the rustle of a gown and a slight touch on the shoulder aroused me from my state of abstraction. It was the young widow, 'the softened image' of the rough old general.

'How do you do, Mr Gernon?' said she, extending her hand with exceeding frankness and smiling cordiality; 'I am so glad to see you again and not looking in any way the worse for your sojourn in Calcutta.' (Oh! that our English pride and sensitiveness, those adamantine trammels of caste, which strangle so many of our virtues, would let us have a little more of that single-hearted openness 'which thinketh no evil'—it is so comfortable!) 'Have you seen my father yet?' asked Mrs Delaval.

I answered in the negative.

'Oh, then,' she continued, 'he will be here immediately when he knows of your arrival, for he is anxious, I know, to see you; he is somewhere in the house, amusing himself with his violin. But pray, Mr Gernon, be seated,' she continued, 'and tell me how you like India, now that you have seen a little more of it.'

'I like it much,' I replied, 'and never was happier in my life. I have got my commission, and as soon as posted to a regiment, am off to the Upper Provinces by water. I have some idea of applying for a particular corps, but have not yet decided on that point: they say you should not interfere with the operations of the Fates, but leave yourself to their direction. What, Madam,' continued I, 'would you advise me to do?'

'Oh! really,' said Mrs Delaval, smiling at the idea of my asking her advice on such a point, 'I fear I am incompetent to advise you, not knowing all the circumstances of your position: you ought, of course, to consider well before you act, and having so done, leave the result to Providence. I am, however,' said she, somewhat seriously, 'a decided predestinarian, and believe that

There is a providence that shapes our ends,
Rough-hew them how we will.'

'It is a puzzling subject,' said I, 'and one that is rather beyond me; one, if I remember rightly, that even bewildered the devils in Pandemonium. However, I think the safest maxim to hold by is, that "conduct is fate".'

This was rather a philosophical opinion for a griffin, but one which I have always held, though young blood at that time and since has often capsized the philosopher.

'Well, Mr Gernon,' continued she, 'you have my best wishes for your happiness and success in life; all is *couleur de rose* with you now; may it ever so continue! Already,' said she, and the tear glistened, 'the clouds of life are beginning to pass over me.'

As' she said this, she crossed her fair white hands on her lap, and the widow's eyes sadly dropped on her wedding ring, the little golden circlet type of eternal fidelity. I understood it, and was silent. Silence is preferable on such occasions, perhaps, to the common-places of condolence. We both continued mute for some moments; she looking at her ring, I out of the window.

At length, I ventured to say,

'Dear Madam, do not deem me impertinent, I pray; but cheer up; remember, as my Irish half-countryman beautifully expresses it, "every dark cloud has a silver lining", and there are doubtless many, many happy days yet in store for you.'

I should have premised, that Mrs Delaval had lately lost her husband, a fine young fellow, who fell in the storm of a small Polygar fort on the coast, and time had not yet brought that balm with which in due course he heals the wounds of the heart, unless the very deepest. I was certainly waxing tender, when the idea of Olivia, my poor abandoned Olivia, crossed my mind.

The widow gave her auburn locks a toss, made an effort at self-possession, smiled through her tears, and was herself again.

'By the bye, Mr Gernon,' said she, 'though but a recent acquaintance, I will assume the privilege of an old friend, and give you some little information whilst we are alone, which may be of some advantage to you in your intercourse with this family.'

I looked alarmed, not knowing what was forthcoming. She perceived what was passing in my mind.

'You need not think, Mr Gernon,' and she smiled, 'that you have come amongst giants or ogres, who are likely to form designs against your life and liberty. Nothing quite so bad as that—no. What I wished to say is, that my father is a man of warm and generous impulses, but violently passionate and eccentric; and I entreat you to be cautious in what you say before him, and do not press any subject if you find him evincing impatience. If he likes, he may serve you; but if he takes a prejudice, he is exceedingly persecuting and bitter: a warm friend, but an inexorable foe. Mrs Capsicum, to much vulgarity adds all my father's violence and irritability, with none of his redeeming qualities. You must be submissive, and prove yourself a "good listener", or you will have little chance of standing well with her.'

This was said with some little asperity of manner, plainly indicating that the stepmother was not more popular than stepmothers generally are.

As for the others you will see here, you may safely be left to the guidance of your own judgement and discretion in your conduct towards them.'

I thanked Mrs Delaval for her information, which, I saw, emanated from the purest feeling of womanly kindness, and promised to be on my guard, and endeavour to profit by it.

The widow and I had not been long engaged in conversation (which, as I before hinted, was becoming rather interesting), when we heard the scrape of a violin outside in the passage.

'Oh, here is my father,' said Mrs Delaval, 'coming from his room. Now remember my caution.'

I was about to reply, but she laid her finger on her lip expressively, as much as to say, 'Another time; he's here.'

The old general now entered, with a black velvet sort of nightcap stuck rakishly on his head, and playing rather jauntily 'St. Patrick's Day in the Morning', to which he hummed an accompaniment—his voice displaying, as usual, all that vigour in its tones which, as I have before remarked, afforded so striking a contrast to his dried-up and time-worn frame: as he entered with his spindle shanks, huge frill, voluminous upper works, pigtail, and velvet cap, I thought

I never saw a droller figure. Still the gallant bearing and nonchalance of the little old Irishman, who evidently was unconscious of anything at all out of the way in himself, rather neutralized any feeling of disrespect which his figure was at first calculated to excite.

On seeing me, he finished off the saint with a few galloping flourishes, pushed the fiddle on the table, transferred the stick to his left hand, and made a rapid advance, or rather toddle, towards me, with his right extended.

'Hah, Sur, I'm glad to see you,' said he; 'Mr Gernon, I believe? Very happy indeed to have your company, Sur; shall be glad to shew you ivery attention in ivery sense of the word, Sur, for the sake 'of my old friend Sir Toby; and I doubt not,' he continued, with a low bow of the old school and a smile, 'that I shall be able also to add, on your own.'

I said, after a hem or two, that I felt deeply obliged for his cordial reception to me, that I should study to deserve his good opinion, and to realize the gratifying anticipations he had so obligingly expressed, &c. &c.

'Ye will, Sur; ye will, Sur,' said the general; 'I've not the laste doubt of it; and plase God, we'll some day see you as accomplished a soldier as was your poor uncle the colonel.'

'What! Sir,' said I, pleased with the discovery; 'did you then know my uncle, Colonel Gernon?'

'Know him!' said the general, with energy and warmth— 'I did, and right well too; we were in Goddard's march together and the Rohilla campaign, and in many places besides. Yes,' he continued, warming as he went on, 'poor Pat Gernon and I have broiled under the same tint and fought under the same banner.'

I felt a sensation of choking, whilst all the ancient blood

of the Gernons mantled in my cheeks, as I listened to the veteran's animated laudation of my deceased relative.

At length on the approach of evening we walked out on the lawn and I paired off with the widow, towards whom I felt myself drawn by an irresistible power of attraction. I felt great delight certainly in the society and conversation of this lady; though then too young to analyse the sources of my admiration, reflection has since shown me what they were, having passed them through the prism of my mind, and separated those pencils of moral light which, united, produced the sum of her excellence. I cannot here resist drawing a little portrait of her.

To a full, yet graceful, person Mrs Delaval united a countenance, which, if not regularly beautiful, still beamed with goodness and intelligence—sensible, lively, yet modest and discreet, she was all that man should desire, and woman wish to be. Above the common littlenesses of the world, her heart was deeply fraught with feeling and sensibility—though, unlike her sex in general, she could direct and restrain them both by the powers of a clear and masculine understanding. Her Irish paternity had given her impulses; her Saxon blood had furnished their regulating power. She played, sang, drew, and, in a word, was mistress of all those lighter accomplishments which serve to attract lovers, but which alone rarely suffice to keep them; to these she added a mind of an original turn, improved by reading and reflection. Much good advice did she impart, the nature of which the reader may readily imagine, and which it will therefore be unnecessary to repeat. It is from the lips of such Mentors, that 'truth' indeed 'prevails with double sway'—one smile from them goes further towards convincing than a dozen syllogisms.

Having, by General Capsicum's promised interest, obtained a fortnight's leave, I went by boat to enjoy a holiday with the General's son, Mr Augustus at his indigo factory.

∾

The day after my arrival at Calcutta I hastened to pay my respects to the Capsicums. On reaching the portico of the house, I threw myself out of my palankeen.

'Is the General at home?'

'He is, *khodabund*,' said the servant, and ascended to announce me. Upon my entering, and making my bow,

'Ha! how are ye, Sir; how are ye, Sir?' said the old veteran, extending his hand to me at full length, as he reclined in his easy chair, 'glad to see you again. Well, Sir, and how did you lave my son? But I've heard of all your prosadings.'

Mrs Capsicum congratulated me on my continued healthy appearance, and condescended to present me with the 'tip of her honourable little finger'.

I looked around for the dear widow, but she was not there. My pulse sunk below zero with painful misgivings; ideas of death, matrimony, or some other misfortune, flashed on my mind: it is the nature of some men always to fancy things fifty times better or worse than they are, to which category I belong. I ventured to ask the general after the health of his daughter, and was greatly relieved by his reply:

'Oh, she's well, sure—she's well; but you'll see her here immediately to spake for herself.'

Some time before dinner was announced, a carriage drove up to the house; it contained Mrs Delaval, who had been absent the whole day in Calcutta. She soon entered the apartment; it was late in the evening, the light dim and uncertain, and I seated in a recess near the window.

'Well, Cordalia, my dear, have you seen all your friends and executed all your commissions?'

Mrs Delaval kissed her father, and answered in the affirmative, adding, 'the Coppletons have taken their passage home in the *Derbyshire*; your Scapegrace, of the civil service, is to be married to Letitia Flirtwell tomorrow, and Colonel Oddfish sends his *bhote bhote salaam* to you, and hopes to see you soon in town.'

After some more gossip of this nature, the general directed the attention of his charming daughter to me, as 'a particular friend of hers', and I had the satisfaction of seeing a blush of pleasure and surprise upon her features at recognizing me.

The reader may readily conceive all that passed, immediately after this and at dinner, and that I had to recount the adventures of the last six weeks, to fight over again the battle of Junglesoor, and to rekill all the hogs.

As the night wore away, and long after tea, the old general, who had been for some time in a ruminating mood—indeed, we had sunk into that thoughtful state which usually precedes the separation of friends—lit his taper, and rising, though with considerable effort, from his easy chair, beckoned me to follow him.

We entered his dressing room; he desired me to shut the door, and sitting down, bade me be seated likewise. He gave me a long sermon on every aspect of life and also sound advice on my future career. In conclusion he said: ''Tis a hard matter, I know, to put an old head on young shoulders; but maybe, nevertheless, you'll sometimes think of what I've now said to ye. And now,' he added with a smile, 'I believe I've finished my sermon, and have nothing more to add, than may God Almighty bless and prosper ye!'

On saying this, the warm-hearted old Irishman, who was evidently affected, applied a key with trembling hand to a little escritoire, from which he took an old-fashioned silver snuff-box. This he rubbed with his sleeve, looking at it wistfully, and then presented it to me, whilst a tear trembled in his eye—the thoughts of other days rushed upon him.

'There,' said he; 'that belonged to your poor departed uncle; forty-five years ago, he gave it to me as a mark of his regard: I now here present it to you as a proof of mine, and in memento of him, the only man on earth I'd give it to before I died. I don't recommend you to snuff yourself generally,' added he, 'but you'll find a pinch in that,' and he smiled, 'that'll do you good sometimes, if used with discretion and sparingly; if you're ever in want of a further supply, let me know; and now, if ye plase, we'll rejoin the ladies.'

I was deeply touched by the general's kindness, and mentally promised that I would treasure up his counsel, and make it my future guide. I fear, however, his estimate, touching that extremely difficult operation of putting an old head on young shoulders, found little in my subsequent career at all calculated to invalidate its correctness.

Well, I bade a long farewell to the general. Mrs Capsicum softened as she bid me adieu, and the charming widow could scarcely conceal her emotion.

How dreary, how blank are the first few moments which succeed the parting with friends! their voices still sounding in your ears, their persons still vividly before your eyes— sounds and pictures to be impressed on the sensorium, and carried with you through life, long, long, perhaps, after the originals are departed!—undying echoes! and abiding shadows!

I reached my room at about twelve o'clock, and prepared

for rest: My first act, however, was to take a survey of my uncle's snuff-box.

It was a singular piece of antiquity, such as might have been handed round in its time at a meeting of wits at Button's or Will's, or tapped by some ruffled exquisite of the glorious reign of Queen Anne. The well-known arms of my family were engraven on the back, but almost obliterated by time and use.

Now, thought I, for a peep at the inside, and a pinch of the general's wonderful snuff. I opened the box, but instead of snuff, I found it to contain, to my great pleasure and astonishment, the following brief, but highly satisfactory document:

GENTLEMEN,—
Please to pay to Ens. Gernon, or order, the sum of Rs. 500, on account of,
Gentlemen, your obedient Servant,
DOMINICK CAPSICUM,
Lieut.-General.

To Messrs. Princely & Co., Agents.

'Generous old man!' I exclaimed, 'such snuff as this is indeed useful at a pinch, though, unlike most snuff, by no means to be sneezed at!'

❧

Well, time wore on; some months had elapsed, during which nothing very particular had occurred, excepting that I received a letter from the charming widow, announcing that my kind friend, the old general, had at last gone to his long home.

It was an admirable epistle, written with all that proper feeling which such an event would naturally call forth in the breast of an accomplished woman and affectionate daughter. It breathed a spirit of resignation, and contained many beautiful, though not very new, reflections touching the frail tenure of existence, and of that inevitable termination of it which is alike the lot of us all.

The general, she said, had not forgotten me in his parting moments, but sent me his blessing, with a hope that I would not forget his advice, and would strive to emulate my uncle, who seemed, indeed, to have been his model of a cavalier.

In conclusion, she stated that she was about to join some relations, who were coming to the Upper Provinces, and hoped she might have an opportunity shortly of renewing my acquaintance, and of assuring me in person, that she was 'mine very truly'.

Yes, mine very truly! I saw I was booked for the widow, and began to put more faith than ever in the Chinese doctrine of invisible attraction. 'Let me see,' said I; 'the widow is two-and-twenty, I eighteen; when I'm two-and-twenty, she will be six-and-twenty. Oh, 'twill do admirably! what matters a little disparity?' So I whistled a *Lillabulero*, after the manner of my uncle Toby, concluding *affettuoso*—

And around the dear ruin each wish of my heart
Shall entwine itself verdantly still.

Reminiscences of Shaik Ismael

British civil and military officers during the Raj led a life of luxury marked by pomp and show. Like the native landed gentry, they employed an army of servants to uphold the supremacy of their establishment. The sahibs and memsahibs were expected to do nothing. There were servants to pull off the sahibs' boots, servants to comb the memsahibs' hair and even to pick up the handkerchief dropped on the floor, as well as a servant for each of their children. Though servants were hired on the recommendation of previous employers, they were not always faithful to their masters. They were in the know of the secret amorous affairs of the sahibs and memsahibs and some of them exploited their knowledge fully.

The following narrative in first person is taken from the East India Sketch-Book *series (1832-33) by an anonymous woman observer of the Indian scene.*

In the name of the Prophet!

My sons, if ye would learn the pathway to plenty and prosperity, even to the attainment of riches, read the recollections of your father, and deposit them in the storehouse of your memory, until the season shall arrive for the planting of the same seed, and, by similar diligence, to the ripening of the same fruit.

I was once, as other men, feeble and without sense. My mother and others about me did with me as they listed. As soon as consciousness dawned, my mother became dearest to me, because I was carried oftenest by her; and even when I had learned the art of walking, I preferred being pillowed on her bosom. Happy is he who can always ride; and happier he who is always still—to whom whatever his wants require, is brought!

This, however, is not the fate of us all. It is written that some must be rich, but many poor. I belonged to the many, and my lot was cast in poverty. I was the son of a sap, and an orderly boy in my father's regiment.

My father died. May his soul be with the Prophet! My mother and myself subsisted entirely on my pay, three rupees each month, as the feringhees (Europeans) count their months. All things were controlled by my mother; and she was wiser than Fatima, the favourite of the Prophet. Whilst our neighbours contented themselves with rice, or on great occasions rejoiced over a vegetable curry, we had daily delicious pilaus, kibaubs, or curries of the choicest meat. We had sweetmeats and fruits also, and my mother possessed saris of the finest cloth. She was young and fair as Zuleika; and her skill in domestic management was wonderful considering her youth. She was often absent from our dwelling; and once or twice, as I was strolling about the streets of the cantonment, I fancied I saw her in the house of a feringhee officer. But she convinced me of my mistake, by reminding me that such a proceeding was quite against her caste. Therefore I ate heartily of the delicacies she set before me, and asked no further questions. Her secret, if there were any, perished with her—peace be on her grave!

As I grew older I attracted the notice of the officers, and

was at length selected by one of them as an attendant. When I first learnt that his choice had fallen on me, in bitter indignation I desired my mother to tell the feringhee, that I was well contented with my present condition, and would be my own master and no man's servant. But my mother was wonderfully persuasive. She set before me how much my future prospects, and all my advancement in the regiment, depended on my consenting to this temporary degradation, as I persisted in calling it; that to refuse would be to stumble on the very threshold; and that a first false step was almost always fatal. Her arguments overcame my repugnance; for how could I refuse to listen to one whose doctrines came recommended by such an illustration of their wisdom, as her own prosperous life?

My new master was an ensign just joined. He was young and ruddy like a pomegranate blossom and had arrived in my country but a few months since. He was filled with all the pride and ignorance of the cafirs (infidels), and often in my heart I spat on his beard, when necessity compelled me to obey his imperious commands.

My mother listened patiently to the recital of all my grievances. She soothed me to present endurance, by the assurance that vengeance always came at length to him who patiently waited for it; and that the slowest poison was often the surest. I obeyed her counsels, and submitted to every infliction in silent and uncomplaining acquiescence. Meanwhile, I laid up in my memory every grievance that was heaped on me, whether by accident or design, in the full and deep resolution that when the day of payment should come, I would exact the debt my tyrant owed me with such an interest as might satisfy the most rapacious revenge that ever burnt in the bosom of one of the faithful.

By degrees, however, as I became fuller of years and discretion, and better acquainted with the manners of the infidel, I learned to conceal enmity under a smooth brow and a smiling lip, and I set myself to learn the language of the cafirs with indefatigable zeal and assiduity. How much I gained by my secret understanding of it! Unmindful of my presence, my master and his friends discoursed openly of their most secret concerns, because Shaik knew nothing! How often my soul rejoiced at thus gaining information of matters of the highest importance! How I triumphed in their security, and rejoiced in the discretion which so carefully guarded my secret from them! Often have I repaid the blows of my master, by spreading abroad tidings of the things which he believed locked up in his own breast, and that of his chosen friend.

Although my profits in the service of my master were tolerable, I was soon acute enough to perceive, that they were not by one-half so great as I might reasonably expect to realize as the butler of an officer married to a feringhee-bibi. Consequently I soon found a pretext for leaving him by kicking a favourite dog, having at first provoked it to attack me, which irritated him so much that he discharged me immediately. I believe on the morrow he would have recalled me, if I had made the slightest submission, but this would not have answered my purpose. So I obtained a written character greatly in my favour, and offered myself to the Major of my regiment, whose butler had just left him, being resolved to return to his own country, which was at Bunder.

In the course of a few days I was installed in my new office, and in a few more had learned exactly the amount which I could contrive to add to my regular pay. My master's wife was extravagantly fond of dress, and the hawkers who arrived at the Cantonment, laden with the refuse of the shops at the Presidency, were sure to dispose of all their gayest stores to her, and her disregard as to the price was just proportioned to her desire of possessing the fine things they exhibited. Of the folly of the English woman was my gain. I never allowed a hawker to approach the house without exacting from him a larger commission than ordinary; and indeed he could well afford it, for my mistress overpaid the value of the goods tenfold. Such, my sons, are the manners of the infidels, who trust so blindly to their wives, deriding our wisdom, who, estimating their weakness and foolishness as they deserve, keep them under wholesome restraint, and find our security in bolts and bars.

I was not long in discovering, that a new source of gain was open to me, if I was discreet enough to turn the opportunity to account. My former master, the young Lieutenant, frequently visited the house of the Major Saib, and his visits occurred generally when the Major was absent. My mother—how she had acquired her wisdom I know not—had frequently endeavoured to open my eyes to the follies of the feringhees regarding their women, so that my suspicions, always on the alert, were very soon excited. I was not long before I was in possession of the whole secret, and I presently contrived that my former master should discover the extent of the knowledge I possessed. His alarm was exactly such as I wished him to feel, and the money he poured into my hand, evinced his desire of securing my silence. Well might he desire it! These misguided Europeans, who allow so much unseasonable liberty to their wives, instead of punishing them for their infidelity, are content to meet in single combat the man who has injured them, placing their own lives in jeopardy, and leaving it to chance whether the husband or the seducer is to suffer the punishment due only to the criminal. Vengenance for every stripe the youth had inflicted on me, was now within my grasp, and though resolved that it should fall on him, I was too discreet to throw away the gains in my power by hastening the time. I promised not only silence but assistance, and he went away from my presence evidently at ease, convinced, as he said, 'that Shaik Ismael would, by his present conduct, prove his gratitude for the favours so long conferred'.

Months wore away, and my hoard was rapidly accumulating from the gifts of the guilty pair. Whether long impunity had rendered them careless I know not, but I saw that the time was drawing near when, if I did not reveal the matter to my master, another would, since I perceived that I was not the only one who knew the fact. One evening, therefore, I threw myself in the Major's way when my mistress was absent in her palanquin, and I thus addressed him:

'Saib, a son of the eagle married a daughter of the eagle, and the son of the eagle, trusting to the blood of his tribe, fearlessly left the daughter of the eagle alone in his nest. But though the nest was built on the top of a rock, the son of the sparrow was able to reach it; and the wife of the son of the eagle, forgetting her husband, in his absence admitted the sparrow to his place in the nest.'

I gazed on the face of the Major as I uttered these words, and I watched his eye expand as he turned it full on me, as if he would search into the depths of my darkest thoughts. I met his scrutiny with a calm front, for as truth was on my side, and I had well weighed the consequence of my communication, I was fearless of any ill to myself. He understood my parable, and he grasped my shoulder tightly, as he commanded me to speak out more plainly.

'I have told all,' said I; 'if the eagle would see the sparrow in his nest, he has but to wait until tomorrow at sunset, and he may trust to his own eyes.'

The Englishman paused a moment, and I watched the secret writhings of the infidel with delight. 'Tomorrow at sunset!' he said at length; 'you have chosen your time ill, sir; now I know you have lied!'

'As master pleases,' returned I submissively, for I knew well which way his thoughts pointed. 'Why should I tell this thing, if I were not sure—why should I bring down anger on myself for that which cannot profit me?'

He mused again. 'Leave me now; I will speak to you in the morning,' said he, and I quitted his presence well satisfied of the result.

The morning arrived, and I stood in the outer veranda where my master appeared ready for the parade of his regiment. His face was so pale that I knew instantly how disturbed a night he had passed; I did not throw myself in his way, but stood aside until he had looked round for me. As soon as his eye fell on me he beckoned me to him.

'By the heaven above us,' said he, 'if I find one word of untruth in what you have told and are still to tell me, this day is the last of your life! To use the words of your own vile fable, at what hour do you mean to say, that the son of the sparrow will visit the nest of the son of the eagle this night?'

'Master is going to have tiffin at the Colonel's,' replied I, glad that his question was so unequivocal; 'after tiffin every gentleman and lady will go to take airing. If master then will come home, he will see with his eyes *the sparrow in the nest of the son of the eagle.*'

He spoke no more, but vaulting on his horse was instantly out of sight.

The intervening hours were full of perturbation. Do not believe that I repented for a single moment the disclosure I had made, or regretted for an instant that the time had arrived, when I was to reap the full measure of my vengeance on the infidel. My anxiety originated in a widely different source. I feared lest some unforeseen event should prevent the interview between my mistress and her lover on this eventful night, and I trembled when I thought on the punishment which, in this case, would inevitably be inflicted on me by my master. Moreover, this was my first step in the pathway of revenge, and, sweet as was the foretaste of its enjoyment, that path swarmed with serpents. However, I reflected that all things were decreed, and resigned myself to the event to which I was destined.

My master and his wife went to the Colonel's according to invitation. When they had departed, I seated myself in the veranda, with my eyes fixed on the western heavens, watching the declining sun. As he sank beneath the horizon, I heard the cry of my mistress's palanquin-bearers. I ran forward to assist her to alight. In a few minutes my old master the Lieutenant arrived, and I retired to a remote corner of the compound to watch the approach of the Major. Every minute, as it passed away, seemed an age to my apprehensions. At length, as I had admitted the belief that some circumstance or other had induced him to disbelieve my story, I saw him approaching, on foot, with that silent step which intimates desire of concealment. I showed myself, and making signs to him to enter, had the satisfaction of seeing him rush into the house.

In a minute—in less—I heard a woman's shriek, and I knew that all was discovered. Concealing myself in a remote corner of the compound, I saw the lieutenant dart forth, whilst my master followed, using violent gesticulations, and uttering loud menaces. The work was done. I knew that my vengeance had been effectually wrought, and that its completion would shortly be effected by other hands than mine. It was! Before sunrise the next morning, my first master lay dead, weltering in his blood.

So slowly and so surely did the revenge of the despised Mussulmaun overtake the cafir that had scourged and scorned him.

And thus the Europeans, who affect to despise our usages, and condemn us for the imprisonment of our women, hold up before our eyes daily proofs of the shame brought on them by their too great confidence in a sex evidently created without any capacity of guiding themselves, and altogether unworthy of trust.

My mistress was sent immediately to her own country, and my master did not remain long with his regiment. He was never the same man afterwards, always gloomy and solitary. I fancy he suffered some foolish remorse for having shed the blood of the man who had injured him. Indeed, I have observed that these cafirs, however they may be bent on revenge, have no satisfaction in looking back on its completion. They are filled with vain compunction, and haunted by a thousand terrors, unknown to a true believer. They seem by the act of vengeance, as if they had, in their own estimation changed places, with the offending party, and I do not believe they have a moment's peace after its perpetration. And yet they bring a hundred petty offences to be decided by mortal combat, which a Mussulmaun receives patiently, and repays fourfold, as I did in the present instance.

❧

My next master was a person very different from any I had hitherto served. Being a man who spoke little, he engaged me without any words, and I entered on my duties very well pleased with the appearance of my new master.

In a short time I found that every thing was under the control of a Moor woman, who stood so high in the Major's favour, that, infact, she was absolute master of him, and of the whole house. I was a long time debating whether I should endeavour to set up an influence opposed to hers, or by bringing her over to desire my aid, add my efforts to hers, and be contented with a share in the pillage, which I soon saw she was carrying on to an extent that startled even me. After much deliberation, for I was too wise to resolve rashly, the latter course appeared to me the most prudent, and I entered on it immediately.

I soon found that the Moor woman was very anxious to discover how my master spent his time when absent from his own house; who were his chief friends, and on what matters they principally conversed together. She knew no language but that of the Moors, and was very glad of the information my acquaintance with the feringhee speech enabled me to give her. I was not long before I entirely gained her favour, and we agreed to share all the profits we were enabled to make under such favourable circumstances. I was sometimes, I must confess, startled at the violence which she showed to the Major when he displeased her; and once or twice I ventured to counsel her on the matter; but she proved to me that she was better acquainted With the art of managing him than I was. Really, when I look back on that part of my life, I cannot help being surprised that an European saib, whose brother-officers all called him a brave man, should submit to the tyranny of the Moor woman so *passively* as he did. I do believe her furious words and looks terrified him, and he was always glad to purchase her return to good humour by a present of money, or of some joy, which pleased her and me quite as well.

At length I heard hints at the mess-table that the friends of the Major—who were more clear-sighted regarding the real state of affairs, so far as concerned the Moor woman, for I was quite unsuspected—were advising him, with all the persuasion they could use, to escape from the trammels in which he suffered himself to be held, by returning to his own country. Laul Bee's rage at the tidings exceeded all bounds, and my utmost influence was necessary to prevent her rushing to the Major's presence, and charging him with harbouring such a design. Shortly, however, my master himself began to throw out hints of such an intention, and to speak of the provision he would in that case make for her. The least glance at the subject was always sufficient to bring on a tempest, and I began to fear, what did in effect happen, that my master would set off so suddenly, that I should not be able to warn her of his design.

For a few weeks he never alluded to his intention of returning home; and even I, with all my anxious observation, was persuaded that he had abandoned it. He began instead to talk of taking a few days' march into the jungle, for the purpose of shooting tigers; and several other officers, some of whom had elephants, were preparing to accompany him. I received orders to prepare everything necessary, and it was not until we had advanced three marches from the cantonment, that I discovered we were actually on our way to the Presidency, whence my master intended to embark, whilst one of his friends was to take charge of his house, and of all the property he had left behind him.

I cannot describe my consternation. All my sagacity did not avail me at this juncture. I was compelled to proceed on my unwilling journey, or to forfeit my wages, and the chance, nay, the certainty of receiving some present from my master previously to his embarkation. I submitted, therefore, to destiny, and we proceeded on our way as rapidly as possible, often making two marches on the same day, and halting nowhere. In vain I indulged the hope of being overtaken by some messenger, or perhaps by Laul Bee herself, in which case I had little doubt that my master would be prevailed on to return; for notwithstanding the violence of this woman, the influence she possessed over him was extraordinary. However, day after day passed, and our progress was not once interrupted. Without accident of any kind, we arrived at the Presidency, and my master engaged a passage in a ship about to sail in a very short time.

I knew that, long before this, Laul Bee was perfectly well acquainted with the real intention of our journey, and that either she had acquiesced patiently in the loss of her prey, or was now on the road in pursuit of him. Earnestly I desired that the latter might be her mode of proceeding; and I hailed every day that my master was compelled to remain, as adding to the chances of her arriving in time to prevent his departure. Alas! all my expectations were in vain. I was compelled to accompany the Major on board; and when the boat brought me back to the land, I stood on the shore, watching the ship as the wind blew it farther and farther away, and bemoaning the destiny which had deprived me of the surest means of wealth that had ever before fallen into my hands.

I prepared to return to the cantonment, and to see how much Laul Bee really possessed, before I took her to be my wife. I did not fear her temper, for I was too good a Mussulmaun to hold women in such estimation as my infidel master had done; and I will engage, with the aid of a good bamboo, to keep the most refractory in subjection. All depended on the amount of her riches, and I had good hopes of finding it such as would form no contemptible addition to my own. The first two marches of my journey were accomplished without incident, but at the end of the third I met Laul Bee herself, *in a palanquin*, having got thus far on her way to reclaim her fugitive master.

How she cursed his beard!—what dirt she threw on him, when she found he was really beyond her reach! I did not escape her anger, and she vowed on the folly which had not prevented his departure. But how long does a woman's rage last? It is like a whirlwind, which blows fiercely and is gone.

The Captain's Betrayal

As it gained political power and prestige the East India Company began recruiting boys in their teens as writers in its civilian establishments in India and as cadets in its armed forces. These were much sought after appointments made by the Company's directors in England. Successful candidates were usually related to them or to their friends. On their departure from England, many young men took vows of fidelity to their first loves with promises of marriage as soon as they had made their fortunes in India. But on arrival in the country they found that things had changed and prospects of getting rich quick were now bleak. Marriage being a costly venture which they could ill afford, young civil and military officers would often forget their 'out of sight' loves and yield to the advances of marriageable girls, especially daughters or nieces of senior officers of the John Company.

This story taken from Mrs Major Clemons's Manners and Customs of Society in India *(1841) is one of unrequited love. A young woman let down by her lover meets a tragic end after her arrival in India.*

Before leaving England to join the East India Company Capt. S—— had become attached to an amiable girl; but he had no fortune or friends to assist him further than getting him his appointment, and giving him a handsome outfit.

The young lady had also no fortune, and her parents refused their sanction to the match, thinking it by no means eligible for her. She was handsome, and highly accomplished, and they considered she could form a better alliance, than marry a poor soldier, doomed to earn a modest living on the burning plains of India. Thus did the parents reason, urimindful of the feelings of their daughter, but not in this manner reasoned Miss A———. She had given her heart to the handsome cadet, and she felt, with all a woman's fondness, that it would never be, recalled. They agreed to correspond, and she waited for many a year, in the hope that he would at last come home and redeem his pledge of fidelity. His letters were frequent and affectionate, and she was as happy as she possibly could be, while separated from him.

On his part, he was gay and lively, and a great favourite with his brother officers.

Though absence had weakened, in some measure, his attachment to Miss A———, yet he considered himself pledged to make her his wife, and fancied that when he attained higher rank, or from ill health was obliged to return home, it would be time enough then to encumber himself with a partner for life. In the meantime, he made himself happy; the time that was not filled up with duty was spent at the mess, or in jovial parties; he constantly affirmed that his heart was in England, and that he should never love any other than Miss A———; he frequently expressed his regret at being absent from her, and his want of fortune, with other impediments, to his marriage. Time passed on; Miss A—lost both her father and her mother. She had had many desirable offers of marriage during their lifetime, but none could fill the place of the absent S——. On the death of her parents, she went to reside with an aunt, who was an old maid, and not one of the most agreeable or estimable of her class.

Now that the poor girl was entirely dependent upon this aunt, she felt that she was far less happy, for she had to put up with many a taunt, and also with many importunities regarding an old bachelor of sixty-three, a rich retired coal-merchant, whom she constantly refused, telling him that she had no heart to give him; and though the aunt still encouraged him to persevere, she as constantly resisted every proposal, and bore the persecution with meekness and patience. S——'s letters were her only comfort. Her own letters to him gradually assumed a more gloomy character. She more frequently reverted to the past days when he was in England, and gently hinted at the hope of his soon returning, as his absence had become unbearable. S—— had been now in India twelve years; he expected shortly to get his company, and he wrote to Emma to beg of her to come out to him at Madras, as it would be too great an expense for him to come to England; adding that the moment he was a Captain, he would send her Pound Sterling 100 to pay for her passage; and, in the meantime, she might get everything ready for the voyage.

On receiving this letter, Emma's hopes revived once more and, her spirits were kept up by the bustle of the preparations, which she immediately commenced.

Her aunt did all she could to persuade her that it was 'highly unbecoming of a young lady to take such a voyage after a man, who, she was sure, did not care a straw for her; otherwise he would have come to England to have married her, or would have sent the money at once for her passage. It was all nonsense; there was plenty of money in India;

everybody was rich there, and had thousands on thousands; it was a most indelicate proceeding, and no one would have thought of such a thing in her day. It was much better to marry Mr Blackton, who had fifteen hundred a year, and such a pretty place at Hampstead, and a nice phaeton and all'. These temptations would not do; poor Emma's mind was made up on the matter.

On the death of her father, she received Pound Sterling 500 which had been placed out at interest, from which she had a small annual income.

The letter from Lieut. S—— had been all that her heart could wish; she plainly saw that it had only been the want of means that had thus long delayed their marriage; and now that he proposed her going out to him, and had assured her there was no impropriety in it, she was determined to draw her little stock of money, pay her own passage to Madras, and thus surprise him by a speedy reunion, fondly hoping that she would, by this step, earlier secure his happiness, as well as her own. It was in July when his letter arrived, and she took her passage in a ship that was to sail in December. In October she received another letter from him, which was as follows:

Madras, June 10.

Dearest Emma, You have no doubt received my letter dated January, and little expected to hear again from me so soon; but my own dear girl will indeed rejoice when I tell her that I was last week in general orders as captain. Now, my love, all impediments to our union are over, and the devotion of my life will, I hope, reward my Emma for her long and faithful attachment to me. I am unable yet to send home the hundred pounds I mentioned in my last letter. I have been at so much unavoidable expense with my promotion, such as buying a new horse which I was obliged to have, and paying the necessary fees for my commission, that I could not possibly do it, anxious as I am to have you with me; but in the course of a few *months*, not years as it used to be, I will send the sum to you, and then embark as soon after as you can,—the sooner, dearest, the better. You must excuse a few lines only, as I intend to write again in a week or two; this was only to tell you the news of my promotion, as I could not be happy and rejoice at it without your participation in my feelings.

Believe me, my dearest Emma,
Your faithful and affectionate
S——

On the receipt of this letter, she was still more satisfied with her determination to take the voyage, and go to him unexpectedly. All was preparation and bustle.

Amidst her aunt's grumblings, a wedding-dress was prepared, and all the paraphernalia necessary for a bride, together with the stock of clothes requisite for a hot climate. At length she embarked: it was in the first week of December. Hope, buoyant hope sustained her amidst the anxiety which could not but be felt at the prospect of her long voyage. We will leave Emma anticipating the pleasure of a reunion with her long absent lover, and take a view of Captain S——.

At the time that he wrote to Miss A——, he meant all he said, though perhaps he did not feel all. A few weeks after he had dispatched the last letter, an English ship anchored in the Madras roads, filled with passengers, amongst whom were the two Miss W——s, daughters of Colonel W——, commanding a station up the country. The colonel and his lady had come down to Madras to meet them on their arrival. He had obtained leave for a month, and had hired a handsome house of a civilian who was just embarking for England on sick certificate. Among other loungers at the breakfast-table of Colonel W—— was Captain S——. He was much fascinated with the eldest Miss W——, and, as he thought himself an engaged man, he perhaps took more licence, and flirted with the ladies oftener than if he had been disposed to win the affections of either of them. Mary W—— was an exceedingly sweet girl, mild and gentle in her manners, and possessed of many attractive accomplishments. Music was one in which she excelled; she had brought out a splendid grand piano with her, and during the month they were at Madras it was unpacked and used.

Captain S—— was passionately fond of music; he sang a little himself, and with Miss W——'s accompaniment, he thought he had never sang so well. He was always to be seen at the colonel's during the heat of the day; and in the evening they generally met at some ball or party. His brother officers began to congratulate him on his conquest, and to tell him he certainly would, through the colonel's interest, obtain a staff appointment. He declared there was nothing in it, that the young lady must see it as well as himself that he only danced with her to save her from disagreeable partners, and that he only went in the morning to, have the pleasure of a little music.

From the continual talk of others, and the constant coupling of their names together, he began at last to think that it would be a good match for him. He saw that other gentlemen always gave place to him that he might be near her. Then he watched her, and evidently saw that her sweetest smiles were directed towards himself; that she always preferred his society to that of others, that a vacant place at the dinner table was always left for him at her side; in short, that both father and mother seemed to think it a match; and that they had no objection whatever he could plainly see, by their manner of welcoming him.

Thus stood matters at the expiration of the colonel's leave. Preparations were hastily made for their march, but still Captain S—— held back. Emma, poor Emma! he would say to himself—yes, he loved her best—but then Miss W—— played so beautifully on the piano!—Emma was handsome when he left her, but then that was thirteen years ago—she would be much changed—besides she was almost thirty years old now—and Miss W—— was about eighteen. He thought that Emma might not care for him so much as she said—he judged her by his own feelings, at any rate— perhaps she would not come out to him, and it was not likely he would ever go home—it would be the best thing he could do to marry Miss W—— at once. With such reasonings and resolutions he went to the coloneys, and made his proposal in form; he was accepted as a son-in-law by both the parents, and was then referred to the young lady herself. It is needless to say that she had bestowed on him her heart, and now willingly granted him her hand.

Colonel W—— applied to the commander-in-chief for another month's leave of absence on account of the marriage of his daughter, which was granted to him. The month that intervened between the declaration and the wedding day, was passed by the young lady in all the preparation necessary for the occasion, and by Captain S—— in restless anxiety of mind, and misgivings as to the step he had taken. He could not banish the thoughts of Emma; in his dreams she was near him as the loved one of so many years—he pictured her as she was when he left England—he reflected on her confiding sweetness, and her strong attachment to him-but the die was cast. The wedding day arrived—and Captain S—— led to the altar Miss W—— that very day in October on which poor Emma received his last letter. In February a change of regiments took place, and Captain S—— and his lady, marched several hundred miles into the interior.

About two months after their departure from Madras, arrived the ship—on board of which was Miss A——. A lady who was coming out to join her husband after a two years' absence on account of her health, had been delighted with the elegant manners and sweet disposition of Miss A——; and Emma on her part was much attracted to the lady, as she was intimately acquainted with Captain S——. Emma made her a confidant, told her little history, showed her the last letter of S——, and dwelt on the pleasing surprise that was in store for him. On their arrival at anchor, the first boat that came from the shore contained Major T——, the husband of the lady, who told him in a few words the story of Miss A——, and expressed a wish, as she had no friends to go to, to take her home, till Captain S—— should be informed of the happiness that awaited him. Major T—— felt horror-struck at this discovery; but said nothing at the time—consented most willingly to protect Miss A—— and thus they landed.

The following day an explanation ensued. It was most reluctantly entered into by the kind major, first with his wife, and then with her friend. The dreadful shock caused by this discovery, was more than Emma's gentle nature could well bear; for several days her life was despaired of; but the soothing affection of Mrs T——, and her own wounded pride enabled her in some slight measure to get the better of her painful feelings. She would frequently say 'Oh! I had much better have borne to hear of his death.' At length she became more calm, and firmly resolved to return to England by the same ship in which she had come out, as it touched at Madras from Calcutta on its homeward voyage.

In the meantime she bent her mind to form some plan for the future. She well knew that her aunt would receive her with scorn; indeed, with her rigid ideas of propriety, she might possibly fancy, that her niece had committed some indiscretion on board the ship, which had prevented the marriage from taking place, and thus refuse to receive her at all. This latter idea took firm possession of her mind; and how to obviate it, became the subject of her anxious thoughts.

She consulted with her two friends, who endeavoured to persuade her to try and shake off her misplaced affection, and not to think of returning to England; but to live entirely with them.

They were then on the eve of marching to Vellore, where the Major's regiment was stationed. Emma would not consent; mildly declined their friendly proposal; but with many tears and thanks accepted their hospitality for a couple of months.

She then came to the decision of writing to Captain S—— to demand a letter from him, stating the reasons for his marriage with Miss W—— at the time that he had sent for her out: in fact giving, as it were, a certificate of her irreproachable conduct, in order that she might with greater firmness meet her aunt on her return to England. The answer to her letter was ordered to be directed to Vellore, for which place they departed the following day. As it may be supposed, her mind was greatly agitated, as each day brought her nearer the expected reply. At last it came; it was full and satisfactory to her present feelings. Thus prepared, she awaited the arrival of the ship; but alas! it came too late, she was attacked with the cholera, and died just six weeks after her landing at Madras.

The Tank Tragedy

Until the middle of the nineteenth century, the demand for European wives far exceeded the supply. Prospective brides belonged to three different classes: daughters of John Company officials stationed in India, their sisters, nieces or near relatives who had been induced to come over and pick up husbands from amongst the large number of eligible bachelors, and the half-caste daughters of mixed unions. 'India is the paradise of middle-aged gentlemen', said a lady writing home from Madras in 1837. This was because young men in India are thought nothing of, being posted in remote areas to make or mar their fortunes; but at forty, when they are high up in the service and somewhat grey, they begin to be taken notice of and called 'young men'. No wonder many girls married men twice or thrice their age who showered them with jewels and costly dresses to win their love. Devoid of attachments, many such unions led to illicit affairs and scandals. Young civil and military officers with no financial means to afford a European wife were ever willing to offer their services and pay their homage to the fashionable married women so inclined. There is mention of a young lady being attended at a Calcutta ball by no less than sixteen admirers, all wearing her colours. The memsahibs' greatest pastime was to meet and gossip about 'who danced with whom, and who is likely to wed,/ And who is hanged and who is brought to bed'.

This tale of love and deceit is taken from the Lays of Ind *by*

Aliph Cheem which ran into several editions during the nineteenth century. It satirizes in verse the love life of the British in India.

Colonel White was over forty;
Jane, his bride, was seventeen;
She was also very naughty,
For she loved a Captain Green!

Colonel White was hale and hearty,
Men are so at forty-nine;
But he was a solemn party,
And he drank a deal of wine.

Every evening, at dinner,
Colonel White would tipple deep,
And that pretty little sinner
Let her Johnny fall asleep.

Then beyond the dark verandah,
In a shady nook unseen,
She would folly and philander
With the wicked Captain Green.

She would tell her darling Gussy,
How that 'sleepy grunting brute'
Called her a disgraceful hussey
When she tried a mild cheroot!

How, when once the corps dramatic
Of the Station sought her aid
Asked her in the 'Dream Ecstatic'
To enact the 'Frenzied Maid'.

He, the monster, in a passion,
Swore he wouldn't let her play—
Said play-going was a fashion
Damnable in every way.

He, for one, had no intention
Men on her their eyes should feast
In a way he wouldn't mention—
('Gussy, wasn't he a beast?')

How he'd not permit her dancing
Anything but dances square—
Called the rest all 'devil's prancing'—
('Gussy, isn't he a bear?')

How he chid her when she joked him,
Slapped her when she didn't heed,
And whenever she provoked him,
Pulled her hair ('he did indeed!')

Beat her with the backs of brushes,
Made her sleep upon the floor—
On, the cruel China rushes—
('Gussy, shall I tell you more?')

How he held the taunt above her—
'If you wish it, cut and run!'—
How there was no one to love her—
('Gussy, is there any one?')

Gussy's answer may be guessed at—
But, for that delicious hint
She so skilfully finessed at,
Gussy had a heart of flint.

Gussy he had no objection
To destroy another's wife,
But a permanent connection—
'Quite absurd, upon my life!'

Mistress White she had an ayah—
'Do whatever Missis please;
Missis send letters by her,
Missis only give rupees.

'Master Green, he handsome master—
Plenty fun-fun, plenty spend—
Never know him when passed her—
Always be that master's friend!'

Once that ayah stole a jewel,
And her mistress-'Ayah say
Missis very, very cruel!'—
Fined her half her monthly pay.

That same day, as black as thunder
Was the solemn Colonel's brow;
And his little wife did wonder
What on earth could be the row.

'Was he cross, the dear old monny!
Was he feeling rather queer
You'll be better, darling Johnny,
When you've had your dinner, dear.'

Then she laid her hand so chubby
On his neck, caressing much;
And she felt her dear old hubby
Shiver underneath the touch.

'Darling Johnny, this is fever;
You had better go to bed.'
And that elegant deceiver
Kissed her Johnny's grizzly head.

Johnny bore the sweet caresses—
Simply said, 'I'm rather weak,'—
While, unseen amid her tresses,
Stole a tear down his cheek.

Dinner came. The Colonel liquored
From the beaker with the lid;
But somehow his eyeballs flickered
Sooner than they mostly did.

Murmured she—'He's weakly, surely—
Something's put him wrong to-day!'
Then the eyelids closed securely,
And the Colonel snored away;

One of them just opened slightly
As the lady softly rose:
Pish!—'t was merely an unsightly
Bluebottle upon his nose.

Swiftly through the dark verandah
Flew she to the nook unseen,
There to folly and philander
With the wicked Captain Green.

'Dearest Gussy, darling, duckey,
I am weary of the strife!
If you love me, and are plucky,
Take me from this wretched life!'

'Jane you turn me tipsy-topsy!—
What's this nonsense in your head?
Think, my precious popsy-wopsy,
Only think what would be said!'

'Do you wish, then, to forsake me?'
'Poppet, can you have a doubt?'
'Gussy, then, oh, why not take me?'
'Cos my wife is coming out!'

'Married?—Oh, you base deceiver!
Monster!—married all the time!
Wife?—Oh, heavens! how 't would grieve her
If she only knew your crime!'

'Can you have a heart, you coward,
Thus to blast her happiness?'
Captain Green's dark eyebrows lowered—
'This,' said he, ' 's a tidy mess!—

'But, my dearest, recollect pray,
You have done the same as I;
Does your Johnny quite expect, pray,
You are here? My love, good bye!'

'Hold!' behind them cried the Colonel—
Captain Green he started back—
'You're a villain most infernal!'
And the rest was, whack! whack! whack!

In the morn, what did they see, oh!
Near a soft and sloping bank,
But that most unlucky trio,
Drowned in an open tank!

Servants said before a jury
That they heard a fearful crash,
Screams for mercy, cries of fury,
And at last a horrid splash!

In the struggle they had stumbled
Over that inviting bank,
And the three together tumbled
Headlong in the fatal tank!

MORAL

He who steals a woman's honour
Is the lowest sort of thief;
Brings all sorts of sorrows on her,
And is bound to come to grief.

She who has a trusting hubby,
And betrays that hubby's trust,
Does an action very scrubby,
And her punishment is just.

He who nails his home's destroyer,
Should not think of using force,
But at once consult a lawyer
That is much the safer course!

The Deserted Husband and the
Criminal Lover

British society in early nineteenth century India, influenced by the Hindu caste system, had developed a hierarchy following more or less the same pattern. Civil officials could be called Brahmins, the highest caste in India. Next in rank came military officers corresponding to Kshatriyas, the Hindu warrior caste. Then followed merchants and traders, counterparts of Vaishyas, who were nicknamed 'boxwallahs' and socially kept at a distance by the first two classes. The fourth class, comparable to Shudras, were the ordinary soldier (Tommies), tailors, barbers, and others. Presentable girls were expected to hook husbands from the top ranks. The achievement of this goal, set by their parents or guardians, involved years of training and brainwashing. The established golden rule to follow was not to lose one's head and get entangled in such a thing as love. There were some who chose to break this rule and found joy and happiness in other quarters.

This tale of a tussle between marrying for money and marrying for love is taken from the East India Sketch-Book series. The author provides an engaging description of the different characters involved in the episode as well as a glimpse into the day-to-day life of the British community.

'Shall I invite Vernon to dine tomorrow?' said Mrs Raymond to her husband.

'Why not? I understood it was to be a general thing,' replied the gentleman.

'Oh, my dear Colonel, that is so like you; forgetting the utter, the complete impossibility of the thing. In that case, we must invite Mrs Slade, you know; and there is *her* sister and *his* to be produced, of course; and they are rather good-looking, I hear—not that I fear their throwing Rose into shade, she is too excessively pretty for that—but distracted attention-that is, *divided* attention, is always injurious; and they say Arnold—the Collector, not the Lieutenant—is rather struck with one. I forget which—and he is so perfectly unexceptionable—and then there is the Resident very desirous of seeing Rose, but fond of music; and Miss Slade plays well, and one cannot avoid asking her to try the new piano. In fact, I have thought it wiser to have only married ladies— Mrs Barney, she squints—Mrs Graham, as dark as an ayah— and Mrs Jones, who is really a perfect female Falstaff, and eats more than two aldermen. So you see, it is by no means general, my love; and one can omit Vernon without being pointed, you know.'

'But what for, Mrs Raymond? You have always so many reasons for what you choose to do, that, confound me, if I can understand one.'

'Depend on it, my dear Colonel, nothing is to be done in this world without proper address; you are so terribly opaque, that you would spoil the best management on earth. However, either I am to act as I please with regard to your niece, or I give up the whole concern; and, moreover, I am positively decided on not inviting Vernon.'

'Once again, why, I ask?'

'Were they not fellow-passengers on board, and is not the voyage the eternal subject of discussion whenever I am so foolish as to allow him to be admitted? And is not Rose evidently quite delighted to talk with him? And have not I seen her neglect other people when he comes up to her as we ride out at night? Very presuming and forward that young man—for a subaltern, moreover, and not on the staff!'

'Precisely my own position when we married, Mrs Raymond.'

'Yes, my dear, true, I was a very foolish young girl then, and had no sound advisers. One gets wise too late: let Rose, therefore, have the benefit of my experience.'

'A thousand thanks, my love.'

'Nay, my dear, I mean no complaint. You must agree with me, that if I did only well, there is no reason why Rose should not do better, and I consider it my duty to try the best for your niece, Colonel Raymond.'

'Very good, my dear; only if, as you say, there should be any attachment between these two young people, Rose and Vernon—'

'I say? Excuse me, Colonel Raymond, this is a very extraordinary charge, and one which I am the last person in the world to deserve. I did, indeed, hint at the possibility of some flirtation existing, which, though the farthest in the world from anything serious, might be in the highest degree injurious to the best interests of our dear Rose. There is a wide difference between a flirtation and an attachment, my dear; but, nevertheless, it may give rise to unpleasant reports, and I must have my way in this point.'

And Mrs Raymond, as usual, not in this point only, but in every point, had her way, and the dinner was given, and Vernon was not invited.

Rose, however, felt his exclusion, and was offended by it: but Mrs Raymond was too well satisfied with her own powers to dread any very unpleasant results from the displeasure of her ward.

Mrs Raymond had three distinct species of vanity— vanity of beauty, vanity of wit—and above all, vanity of management. She piqued herself on an air spiritual, which gave a charm, she conceived, to sharp, keen, and irregular features.

Mrs Raymond had her party, and Vernon was absent. The table groaned under the plenty of an Indian dinner, and glittered with its costliness. Nevertheless it was a very dull party, passing the dulness of Indian entertainments generally. The Resident talked of Miss Slade's playing, and the Collector toasted Mrs Slade's sister, and Rose was in the sullens, and quite impracticable. She made no impression, that was evident; and, as Mrs Raymond justly said, 'the party was evidently thrown away'.

Mrs Raymond had too much tact to notice her niece's dissatisfaction, far less to attribute it to Vernon's absence. She never attempted by any overt act to restrain the freedom of her intercourse with him, and when he called she received him with that frank friendliness which she extended to all her acquaintance, never perceptibly distinguishing the superior rank, which really formed the passion of her soul, if she had a soul. Rose was young, flexible, never of very strong mind, and educated for India. She liked Vernon passing well, and any manifestation of opposition to her attachment on the part of her protectress might have had the effect of confirming that attachment. But she had been taught to place a high value on position, and the luxuries that attend large incomes and superior rank. She had not strength of mind sufficient to face the severe economy which must mark a subaltern's life, or condemn him to perpetual debt and exile. She flirted with Vernon, without any intention of marrying him, and accepted at length-thrice happy moment of Mrs Raymond's ambition—Mr Arnold, the Collector, who had been scorched beneath five-and-twenty summer suns in India, without any worse effects than liver, corpulence, and saturnine complexion.

Vernon thought himself jilted, and was highly indignant. But these more violent emotions soon die a natural death in a tropical climate. Mrs Arnold was quite the fashion; she gave magnificent parties, sported superb equipages, carriages, elephants, luxuries both of the east and the west; received visitors of all classes with amiable good temper; and, Vernon resolving also to visit her, commenced a flirtation at the house of a mutual acquaintance, and from that moment the affair was *en train*.

It was very soon a matter of course, that Mrs Arnold should be driven every evening in a curricle Vernon sported just at this time, to the great scandal of the field-officers of the station. He must be involving himself very deeply, they said; no subaltern could afford two horses in addition to his riding-horse. He might wait six or eight years for his company yet, and in the meanwhile his debts would be increasing to a fearful magnitude. And what in the world was Arnold doing? Was he blind, and could not see? or deaf, and could not hear, what all the world were talking about? And where were Mrs Raymond's wits? Had she lost her acuteness and penetration, which she was everlastingly employing in affairs that did not concern her? It was a great pity her faculties, which were so constantly directed to the benefit of the universe at large, were not a little more useful in the guidance of her own connections. It was really to be lamented that she had chosen the precise time for napping, when it was most requisite that she should be wide awake.

Mrs Raymond did awake at length, and she set herself to divert the current of affairs with all possible address. The result was the following note.

My dear Rose,

Will you be at home and quite alone, this morning, at noon precisely? I wish to pass an hour with you *tête-à-tête*, if you can spare me so long. You know that I am not a very formidable personage, and you cannot, therefore, refuse me on the ground of alarm.

Yours, very much,
Jane Raymond.

To which the following answer was returned.

My dear Mrs Raymond,

I should have the greatest delight in receiving you as you propose; but Vibert, the artist, is to have a sitting from me just at the hour you mention, and Mr Arnold is anxious that my portrait should be completed without delay, as V. quits this very shortly. Any other time, if I am fortunate enough to be disengaged, I shall devote an hour to my dear Mrs Raymond, without any alarm, and with the greatest pleasure.

Yours, affectionately,
Rose Arnold.

Now Mrs Raymond had not exactly calculated on being refused; so, as she could not obtain the interview she desired, she made her call at noon nevertheless, and contrived to be present during the whole of this sitting. Vernon was one of the guests; but as Mr Arnold himself was also there to superintend the efforts of the artist, and amiably unconscious that any other person was at the same time superintending the appearance and attitude of the exceedingly pretty original, Mrs Raymond thought she could not very plausibly mention the circumstance to Rose, as objectionable. At length the sitting was over, and there seemed to be a tacit struggle between Mrs Raymond and Mr Vernon to compel the other to depart. At length the lady invited herself to tiffin; but as the gentleman was very quickly and quietly seated at the hospitable board, it seemed evident that his presence there had been expected. Mrs Raymond finally was compelled to beat a retreat, being for this time completely out-generaled.

Mrs Raymond had always given her niece credit for the greatest possible simplicity and facility of character. She calculated on her being pliant to the influence of a superior mind—as the osier to the wind. But she forgot that woman's first attempt at concealment is the first admission of the serpent into Eden. She felt herself constantly baffled in all her attempts at gaining a *tête-à-tête* with Rose; but she had no cause of complaint. Mrs Arnold always received her visits with the greatest pleasure, indeed with an unusual appearance of affection—but then she was never alone, not for one minute, whilst Mrs Raymond remained with her. Finding, therefore, her progress completely obstructed in this direction, she turned, like a person to whom all routes are equal that conduct him to his destination, into a different path.

Colonel Raymond received her first hints of the matter with ridicule and positive incredulity. But the mere repetition of an assertion, unassisted by any additional weight of evidence, goes far to enlisting our faith on its side. When once he was sufficiently wrought on to view the subject as serious, he saw enough to corroborate all Mrs Raymond's assertions; and he felt, more deeply than she did, all the misery that threatened Rose, because he had no ambition of displaying his own cleverness, or of introducing himself amongst the characters of the scene as an adviser, a judge, or an avenger. Moreover, he had a very deep feeling of the shame and dishonour that shrouds an erring wife, notwithstanding his long absence from Europe, and he thought no risk too great, no action too hazardous, to prevent the fixing of so tremendous a stigma on the child of his brother. He was a very straight-forward person, and it struck him that the individual most concerned in the business was the husband, who was likely to be the severest sufferer. He, therefore, decided that his best plan would be to go quietly and directly to Mr Arnold, and advise his cutting Mr Vernon dead with all convenient speed.

Mr Arnold was aghast. Supine, from the effect of long residence in India, and from his habitual yielding to the climate, he had been satisfied with seeing the very beautiful face of his wife clothed in constant smiles; with hearing her cheerful laugh, and with a splendid dinner, and surrounded with lively guests. He thought Vernon an excellent fellow, and was well pleased that Mrs Arnold shared this feeling. If she preferred Vernon's curricle to her own carriage, he saw no reason why her preference should be opposed. If she selected him as her cavalier at a ball, as her *escorte hither* and *thence*, well and good; it saved her husband the annoyance of accompanying her, and the disagreeableness of teasing her by keeping her at home. No husband on earth could be more indulgent. It seemed as if the chief gratification his large income afforded him, was to administer to her taste for jewels and equipages, and those delights which are generally most coveted by the young. He was pleased to be considered by her the very kindest being of her acquaintance, and he received her lively thanks for every fresh proof of his attachment, with the fond delusion that they originated in that mingling of love and gratitude which constitutes, probably, the best principle of conjugal affection. And now to be so rudely awakened to be told that he might possibly be a dupe, the dupe of a mere girl, whom he petted as a plaything, and whose nature he had deemed as guileless as that. of the just-fledged bird that makes its first flight from the parent nest! Mr Arnold was completely overcome; an instant sufficed to convert the 'milk of human kindness' with which his heart abounded into gall. His vehement indignation assumed a character the more formidable from his general state of quiescence and equanimity. It was long before Colonel Raymond could persuade him to adopt such measures as were necessary at once to secure his wife's virtue and her reputation. He condemned the Colonel, Mrs Raymond, and himself, for their blameable blindness; he execrated Vernon for his meditated sin against every law of morality, every bond of hospitality; he alternately exaggerated and extenuated the weakness, the meditated ingratitude, of his wife. But the stormy mood exhausted itself at length by its violence; and when the Colonel left him, he was satisfied that he would immediately adopt that course of conduct which was most likely to result in the preservation of his honour, and the redemption of his happiness.

Mrs Raymond was perfectly *enragée* that the Colonel had ventured on this important step without asking her advice or opinion. She flung from him in a fit of high disdain, and dispatched instantly the following missive to Rose, in the persuasion that she was actuated merely by the benevolent feeling of apprising her of the exact situation in which she stood.

> My dear Rose,
> I have in vain endeavoured for some time to give you a hint of the various rumours that are in circulation, not only through the cantonment, but in fact throughout the Presidency, of your violent flirtation with Mr Vernon. You have so perseveringly avoided any confidential communication with me, that I am at last driven to this very unsafe method of conveying to you intelligence which, perhaps, will now reach you too late. I have no leisure for preparation, and it is not expedient to delay. In a word, Mr Arnold is in possession of some fact connected with you and Mr Vernon, which will probably lead to an immediate *eclaircissement*, for which my desire is to give you warning to prepare yourself. What may be the real state of the case you only can be aware. At any rate, to be taken quite unawares, might elicit some sudden disclosure, which it would be prudent to avoid and which might enlighten Mr Arnold more perhaps than would be desirable; if, indeed, of which I am by no means certain, anything remains unknown. Prepare yourself.
>
> Yours, very truly,
> Jane Raymond

In the evening of that day the whole cantonment was in a state of agitation. Mrs Arnold had quitted her husband's house, and was actually living in Mr Vernon's quarters.

The next circumstance to which public attention was directed was a duel between the deserted husband and the criminal lover. The whole proceeding was conducted with the greatest regularity. There was nothing that could possibly be construed into the slightest tincture of unfairness in either party. But Mr Arnold found his satisfaction in death, and Mr Vernon honourably added the character of murderer to that of seducer and adulterer.

That the guilty Mrs Arnold endured in her first feelings of anguish the measure of the Divine vengeance on her crime, may be imagined; but naturally of a temper that skims only the surface of things, she was not long without the alleviation that disposed to attribute the whole affair to Mrs Raymond's violent proceeding—to the foolish chit which had brought on a crisis neither she nor Vernon had ever before contemplated very distinctly. Then she went back to her marriage—her *forced* marriage she called it, overlooking the trifling circumstance of its being entirely the result of her own free-will;—*if* she had been permitted to marry Vernon! *if* she had not been over-persuaded! *if* she had not been terrified by representations of the privations to which the wife of a subaltern was exposed—representations too so greatly exaggerated! And thus she laid the flattering unction to her soul', until she brought herself to receive Colonel Raymond with composure.

The Colonel felt as a man on whose honour a stain had been cast by the misconduct of a person so nearly connected with him; he felt also, as a friend, the death—the sudden, the awful death, of a being he had esteemed. Neither was he insensible to the evils of poverty, and obscurity, and disgrace, to which his most criminal niece had exposed herself. He expected to see her overwhelmed with remorse—subdued by repentance—sinking beneath the despair of the dark future. He came prepared to speak words of comfort; to offer protection—a shelter in England, the relief of competence to obscurity. He meant to say, 'Sin no more,' and to offer the means of preservation. The reception of him was naturally an agitated one. 'Some natural tears she dropped, but wiped them soon;' she discussed every topic calmly—spoke of the future with something approaching to cheerfulness— condemned the whole of Mrs Raymond's proceedings most unscrupulously—extenuated all her own share of the transaction, and represented herself as the victim of her aunt's too great love of controlling everybody, and managing all the world. Poor Colonel Raymond was completely overwhelmed by finding her in a state of mind so contradictory of all his anticipations. He had arranged his mind for offering consolation, and he found himself the person who most needed it. However, the Colonel did not suffer his indignation to counteract the designs of his benevolence: with recovered composure he steadily advised Mrs Arnold to proceed to England forthwith—to have no fear of a provision for the future, because, having been the cause of her being brought to this country, and having advised the marriage that had been dissolved under circumstances so awful and painful, he held himself bound to care for her future provision.

Mrs Arnold was quite astonished that the Colonel could contemplate any other line of conduct for Mr Vernon and herself than a marriage as soon as possible. She did not doubt they would be able to exist comfortably: she did not require splendour; and if the people of the cantomnent did not choose to visit her, she could exist without them: and then Vernon would soon get his company; and when he was a major, he would pay his debts, and, on the whole, she was sure they should get on very well as soon as this misfortune was a little forgotten.

'You cannot forget—you will never forget that Mr Vernon is your husband's murderer!' said the Colonel, provoked into severity.

'It was all quite fair; and if one were to call every duellist a murderer—!' She burst into tears.

Colonel Raymond distinguished between the agitation of grief and that of passion.

'I have but one word to add,' said he: 'to waive all suggestion of the impropriety of a marriage under your circumstances—Vernon is under arrest, and will as surely be dismissed as he will be tried by court-martial: he will have no means of supporting you; and I tell you, Rose, very plainly, that you have nothing to rely on but the plan I offer. Suppose your marriage with this man were to take place, and our connection, our intercourse, cease for ever? Take time to reflect, and let me have your answer tomorrow.'

Whether she was capable of reflecting may be doubted; however, she did marry Mr Vernon.

As Colonel Raymond had predicted, he was dismissed from the service. An income of one hundred and fifty pounds yearly, the recent bequest of his father, whose death had been hastened by the report of his son's misconduct, was their sole earthly resource: they retired to France, and remained there in what degree of comfort might be conjectured, by reflecting that Vernon had, for ten years, been accustomed to Indian habits and indulgencies—that his wife was educated entirely with a view to visiting India on a matrimonial speculation, and was as vain, shallow, and thoughtless, as a woman of that class might be imagined—

that she enjoyed the luxuries of Colonel Raymond's house on her first arrival in the East, and subsequently was surrounded by all the expensive comforts and superfluities which affection could lavish round her. No rational person could doubt that their lives were spent in a succession of reproaches, repentance, privation, and disgust—all that makes this world a type of that more fearful judgement which is to constitute the darkness of a future one.

Madame Grand's Great Passion

The post-Plassey period which lasted until the last decade of the eighteenth century was the golden age of corruption and licentiousness for the British in Calcutta. It thrived on scandals and gossip about the liaisons of the ladies which were reported in the Bengal Gazette. *Fashionable, attractive women, both single and married, drew attentions from hordes of admirers, flamboyant and eccentric sahibs in the lead. Wealth, leisure and climate encouraged drinking and debauchery. Even the high-ups cared little for moral values. Warren Hastings, the first Governor General, himself set a poor example by living openly for years with the wife of Imhoff, an impoverished German portrait painter, and then celebrating his marriage with the 'alluring adulteress' with great rejoicing. The most juicy scandal, however, was about one Philip Francis and Madame Grand, daughter of a French official at Chandernagore. Madame Grand, née Catherine Werlee, had been married at the age of 15. Her captivating beauty caused a sensation in Calcutta, attracting a string of admirers. After her adventurous career in India, she sailed alone for Europe. Not missing another opportunity of having an affair on the voyage with one Thomas Lewin, she eventually ended up as Princess Talleyrand, hostess to statesmen at the Congress of Vienna.*

The story of Madame Grand's romantic adventures is drawn from British Social Life in India, 1608-1937, *by Dennis Kincaid*

(1938), a most comprehensive treatise on the subject. A book of much historic value and human interest, it gives a vivid description of the changing pattern of British social life in the metropolitan cities and the mofussil with the increase of their wealth and power.

There were few bachelors as fortunate as Francis who installed his French mistress in a great house at Hooghly to which he would drive out from Calcutta either with a party of friends, or alone for a quiet week-end. There, with his discreet cousin, Baggs, who acted as dragoman, and with the enchanting Madame Grand he would rest after the ardours, intrigues and faction-violence of Calcutta. These pleasant hours would be recorded with brief sighs of satisfaction in his diary. 'Sunday. At Hughely. *Ridet hoc inguam Venus ipsa, rident simplices nymphae.*'

The first husband of this lady, the unfortunate Monsieur Grand, was of a Huguenot family with English connections. He was educated at Lausanne and then sent to London where he was apprenticed to Mr Jones of Lombard Street. Mr Jones welcomed him brusquely on his arrival, 'and asked me if I had brought him any cheese, which being answered, seemed to work a happy change'. Nevertheless he made Grand sleep in the same bed with a footman and crop his hair in order that 'people might not take him for a French monkey'. Luckily his aunt, who had influence at India House, procured for him a cadetship in Bengal. He stayed with Hastings who took some interest in him and despatched him to Chandernagore with a letter of introduction to the French authorities. There he met Mdlle Werlee whose 'fine blue eyes with black eyelashes and brows gave her countenance a most piquant singularity'. He married her and brought her to Calcutta where her beauty caused a sensation. Francis met her at a ball and wrote in his diary: *'Omnia vincit amor.* Job for Wood, the salt agent.' A month later Francis tried to break into Mr Grand's house while the husband was at supper with Mr Barwell. A servant broke in upon the supper party and whispered in agitation to Grand that Francis had been caught in his garden apparently trying to break into Madame Grand's bedroom. Grand burst into tears and raced home to find in his garden not Francis as he had expected but Mr George Shee, a relation of the noble Burke, held down by a posse of servants. The servants explained that while they were holding Francis a rescue party had scaled the wall and set Francis free. They had, however, managed to secure a member of the rescue party.

Francis pretended to be astonished at the uproar that followed. He dismissed his escapade as a 'wretched business' as though it was as ordinary a nuisance to find a Member of Council attempting an assault on one's wife as to discover a grass-snake in the bathroom. But Grand was out for blood. He filed a suit against Francis, claiming 1,500,000 sicca rupees as damages. His counsel was Sir John Day, whose knighthood, bestowed by the King shortly before he sailed for India, had inspired George Selwyn to a typical quip. 'By God, this is out-heroding Herod. I have long heard of the extraordinary power His Majesty exercised, but until this moment could not have believed that he could turn Day into Knight and make a Lady Day at Michaelmas.' Francis was defended by Tilghman, of whom he remarked, enthusiastically, 'His principles are truly patriotic, especially when in liquor.' But the evidence was black against Francis. Miran, a table-servant, deposed to the discovery of a bamboo-ladder against the house-wall. He called the other servants. While they were talking Francis emerged from the house. He was startled at seeing the servants and said hastily, 'I will give you money. I'll make you all great men.' They closed round him whereon he began to bluster, 'Don't you know that I am Mr Francis? Why, I am the Great Sahib.' But in spite of this they seized him. The servants corroborated each other with remarkable accuracy. Tilghman's cross-examination was singularly feeble. He tried to confuse the servants by searching questions about the exact hour of the offence—a favourite trick of English lawyers in India which, as a matter of fact, never impresses a court favourably, since judges know well enough that Indian witnesses have little sense of time—and often no acquaintance at all with the English hours. Unshaken by Tilghman's inquisition, the servants described the arrival of the rescue party, Francis's escape and their capture of Shee. They nearly captured another rescuer but he managed to free himself. This rescuer turned out to be Ducarel, another of Francis's parasites. Everybody began wondering how he could have escaped while Shee remained prisoner. For Ducarel, a serious-minded person interested in science and in the problem of personal immortality, was a dwarf. He was treated as a jester and buffoon by Francis who once addressed a letter to him beginning 'You d——d old fool'. So when this unfortunate creature appeared in the witness-box one of the first questions addressed to him was how he escaped. The dwarf drew himself and replied, 'Finding myself pressed, I offered, amongst other expedients, three gold mohurs.' In other respects, however, he was driven to admit the whole of the prosecution case; and even acknowledged that he had watched Francis creeping down the lane outside Mr Grand's house, carrying the very same ladder that was found in Mr Grand's garden and was now produced in court.

During the hearing there occurred the continual wrangles

over the spelling of witnesses' names that seem to have been inseparable from the procedure of British courts of that period. There were lengthy discussions on law, for one of the three judges, Sir Robert Chambers, never missed an occasion for eager but largely irrelevant legal disquisitions. He was a sharp-tempered judge and during the hearing of an earlier case had referred to the plaintiff's attorney as 'a gentleman probably heated with wine'. Whereupon the attorney, as though to prove his sobriety, leapt to his feet and shouted at the judge, 'You are a contemptible animal.' No such incidents marked the hearing of the Grand case but the interminable discussions, the citing of rulings, the hitches and interruptions, must have been exasperating to Francis who was notorious for his contempt of lawyers, and could hardly utter the word 'attorney' without an insolent and wounding sneer. In this he only followed the fashion of the day. For lawyers were perhaps the most unpopular members of the English community in Calcutta, and the papers were full of gibes at them, such as the following 'Epitaph':

> God works wonders now and then
> Here lies a lawyer and an honest man.

Answered:

> This is a mere law quibble, not a wonder,
> Here lies a lawyer and his client under.

Or this epigram: 'The attorneys of Calcutta may be said to be to lawyers what apothecaries are to physicians, only that the they do not deal in *scruples*.' Nor was even the Advocate-General spared; for when he quarrelled with his assistant and nearly fought a duel, the failure to meet in accordance with the tradition of gentlemen was satirized in this couplet:

> *If the astonishing account is true,*
> *They met, they talked, they drew—and they withdrew.*

The trouble was that while many of them were respectable citizens their numbers were swelled by persons of dubious antecedents, dismissed surgeons or officers convicted of 'an error of judgement'—such as the notorious Hall of Madras who in the war with Hyder Ali was responsible for the loss of 500 men and three guns, which loss caused his commanding officer to succumb to a bilious attack 'which prevents me being so explicit as I otherwise should have been'.

The day of the Grand trial, however, the men of law had their revenge on their most violent critic, Francis, for not only did the examination of witnesses drag on and on, but when all the evidence had been heard the judges differed; which necessitated each giving his separate opinion. Mr Justice Hyde as junior spoke first and treated the matter as one concerned solely with appreciation of evidence and gave it as his opinion that the plaintiff had established his case. Sir Robert Chambers then spoke at enormous length, confining himself to the legal aspects of the suit. He was at last interrupted by the Chief Justice, Sir Elijah Impey, who 'petulantly observed that he was not prepared to comment upon such a mass of learning in Ecclesiastical Law as had been, he thought unnecessarily and inapplicably, introduced by his brother Chambers, not a particle of which applied to the present case'. He agreed with his brother Hyde and entered judgement for the plaintiff, the suitable damages being, in his opinion, 50,000 rupees. Mr Justice Hyde had fallen asleep during Sir Robert Chambers's remarks, but as the Chief Justice announced these damages he woke up with a start and said anxiously 'Sicca rupees, brother Impey, siccas.' 'Aye,' said the Chief Justice with relish, 'Let them be siccas, brother Hyde.'

The Chief Justice's censures on the conduct of Francis and his rescuer Shee inspired a number of pasquinades, of which the following is typical:

> *Psha! what a Fuss, 'twixt SHEE and 'twixt her!*
> *What abuse of a dear little creature,*
> *A GRAND and a mighty affair to be sure,*
> *Just to give a light PHILIP (fillip) to nature.*

> *How can you, ye prudes, blame a luscious young wench;*
> *Who so fond is of Love and romances,*
> *Whose customs and manners are tout a fait French,*
> *For admiring whatever from FRANCE-IS!*

But Madame Grand retired from the curious glances of Calcutta drawing-rooms to Francis's house at Hooghly. After some time, she visited England and stayed at Fitzroy Square with a Mr Lewin. She had saved a comfortable sum which she invested in English banks; and when she finally returned to France she was careful to leave her money behind in England. The Revolution thus caused her little concern. But when she learnt of Napoleon's proposed invasion of England she was filled with horror. She visited the Foreign Minister and implored him to promise that the London banks should not be pillaged. M. de Talleyrand was fond of pretty women and presently Francis's mistress became Madame de Talleyrande and Princess of Beneventum. Thereafter she seems to have lived prudently and the only whisper of her former glamour that survived her marriage was Napoleon's confidence that she would seduce the Prince of the Asturias at Valengay.

Marriage, a Take-in on Both Sides

*Around 1800, there were 250 European women in Bengal and its
dependencies against 4,000 male inhabitants of respectability
including military officers. There was in this situation little scope
for a junior company officer with limited financial means to acquire
a European wife. Many of them therefore attached themselves to
'native' women or looked for well-to-do spinsters or widows. Some
even waited for five to six years to earn leave to be able to go home
to find a wife. In order to meet the deadline of the return passage,
some even opted for arranged marriages. There is a delightful
account by Lt. Thomas Bacon of the adventures of one Charles
Howard whom he had met during his voyage to India in 1881. An
Ensign (Sub-Lieutenant) in the Company's army, Howard had in
his own words posed as a Captain in the London marriage market
to win the hand of a wealthy widow, who turned out to be as broke
as he was!*

Lt. Thomas Bacon in the Preface to his two-volume memoirs,
First Impressions and Studies from Nature in Hindostan
(1837) declares that 'the author pledges himself to the public that
none of the contents of these volumes are fictitious'. He extends
this pledge to the characters and adventures recorded in them.
Referring to the story of Howard, reproduced ahead, he says: 'This
might be objected to as a fiction, on the ground of its improbability,
but it is true, or as nearly true as a relation by a second party will

admit.' The story has been written in the form of a first person account by Howard.

On my return to England, after four years' slavery in India, I found my family rusticating in the vicinity of a small watering-place, instead of living, as I had known them, in all the gay doings of the West-end of Town. My sisters— the two pretty ones at least—had fetched their price in the London market, and as there was no chance that the one left upon the shelf would ever be disposed of, my prudent parents had sought a rustic home, for the sake of husbanding the scanty remnants of a once ample income. This dull secluded sort of life was anything but palatable to me, as you may guess; so I speedily framed an excuse for visiting the metropolis. There I soon found out some of my old friends, and among others was warmly received by Lady A., a gay widow, somewhat past her prime, but retaining traces of her former beauty.

A few days after my arrival in town, I received an invitation to a fete at Lady A's, Everything was in the first style; the room magnificently furnished, and brilliantly attended by a crowd of exclusives. The first person who particularly attracted my attention was a lady, sitting upon the left of our hostess. She was, indeed, a lovely and most striking woman; she was attired in deep mourning, and her simple, but at the same time rich costume, was beautifully contrasted with the elaborately gay attire of the lady next her.

So completely was my admiration fixed by this lady, that I hesitated in my manner as I approached to pay my devoirs to the lady of the mansion. Lady A. received me most cordially, and immediately introduced me to her companion as an old and valued friend, and then moving to another part of the room, she left me to entertain the beauty. I do not know that she could strictly be called beautiful; she was in every respect comely, but it was the eye which gave such a magical witchery to the countenance. I never before had seen such eyes: they were those long, dark, flashing, yet languishing eyes, which tell all that they are told to say, in infinitely more touching language than tongue was ever schooled to; her hair was of that dark brown so nearly black, and, in keeping with the simplicity of her costume, was dressed *a la vierge*; her figure was somewhat of the tallest, but perfectly elegant and easy; and then the foot—oh! such a foot—was peeping from the flowing gown, now extended, now withdrawn; she herself could not help casting an occasional glance of admiration at it; words could not have spoken more plainly, 'find me its equal!'

'I had formerly the pleasure, Captain Howard, of an acquaintance with your family and sisters, but lately I have heard nothing of them.'

I explained that they had retired into the country, and then again looked silently down at her pretty foot; it was protruded a very little further from the dress, and the slender fingers slyly and under cover of the embroidered handkerchief, drew the skirt a thought higher up the ankle; an ankle that Venus herself would have envied. She evidently observed the impression which she had made, but I was not the boy to be long taken aback, and quickly began to exert myself for her amusement. It is not for me to say that I was successful; but when I asked her to dance, she replied, 'I have already declined several requests; however, my headache is somewhat better, now: but I detest quadrilles; we will waltz.'

I will say nothing of how my cheek flushed and my heart bounded, as I supported my partner through the circling mazes of the waltz; I don't know whether my brain whirled most with intoxicating love, or the giddy dance. After handing the lady to her carriage, having dangled in her train all night, I mentally exclaimed, 'Well, I little thought that I should ever be inclined to wed; but, if devotion, stratagem, or compulsion, can make that woman Mrs Howard, why Mrs Howard she shall be: that is, if she has any money of her own—ten thousand would do; ay, or five, with such a foot and ankle as that: if she has nothing, why of course it is out of the question: couldn't even afford a cab to take her to church.' I hastened back to the half-deserted rooms to bid adieu to our hostess.

'Well, my young friend,' said she, 'is not Mrs M. a sweet young creature?'

'Oh, an angel. Has she any fortune?'

'Twenty-five thousand, and in her own right,' whispered Lady A.

'She's a perfect little divinity.'

I had obtained my siren's address, with permission to call the next day; and one o'clock found me, with a nervous hand and heightened colour, vainly endeavouring to please myself at my toilet.

"Tis true,' thought I, 'the twenty-five thousand may depend upon the tying of this cravat;' so, after soiling half a dozen, I became desperate, and screwed it up anyhow, in a state of nervous anxiety and excitement, for which there was no occasion. I was just sallying forth from my door, to walk to the residence of my fair inamorata in Cavendish Square, when Lady A.'s carriage drove up, and the servant handed me a three-cornered pink note. What a bore, thought I, half aloud, as I commenced reading:

My dear Captain Howard,
I know you are very seldom disengaged, but if you
do happen to be at leisure, pray jump into my
barouche. I am going shopping, and want your
judgement upon some India shawls.
In haste, & c.
Louisa A.

'Tell your mistress that you met me from home, that I regret
I am unable to attend her, being engaged upon most urgent
business.' While giving this message, I was folding up the
embroidered note, and discovered the following brief P.S.:
'Mrs M. is with me.' I cut short my speech, ordered the
servant to open the carriage-door, jumped in, and in a fever
of expectation, gave the man his order, home.

With just sufficient leisure to build a whole city of
castles, I arrived at Belgrave Square: taking three steps at a
stride, I was quickly in the presence of the two widows. I
entered unannounced, and my own name was the first word
which fell upon my ear. My abrupt entry somewhat
disconcerted them for a moment.

'Ah, Captain Howard,' exclaimed Lady A.; 'this is really
kind of you: here are we two forlorn widows obliged to beg
for a beau. I was apprehensive too that some other
engagement might have debarred me the pleasure of your
society.' This was said with an arched brow, and a slight
shrug, which shewed she knew whither I had been engaged.
Of course I assured her ladyship that no engagement could
possibly interfere with my obedience to her commands. A
look from the other lady said, 'Faithless fellow, you were to
have, called on me.' Here was a pretty scrape; however, no
explanation could be made, and away we went to the shawl

merchants. With increasing intimacy, I gained confidence, and did not at all despair of ultimately succeeding to the pretty little white hand and twenty-five thousand. Lady A.'s assurances were most encouraging, and besides she warranted the validity of the fortune.

It is not to be supposed that I was the only suitor for the hand of this sweet lady and her cash—four or five other followers had enlisted in her train; but I had too much vanity, and too much encouragement from Lady A. to distress myself about them individually, although so circumstanced as to be apprehensive of crushing all my own fair projects through want of time to bring them to a head.

In order to follow the pursuit with a prospect of success, I had deemed it expedient to live in better style than I had the means of supporting, and upon the chance of the twenty-five thousand. I had been induced to run into all kinds of extravagances. My creditors, finding that they could obtain nothing better than promises from me, became exceedingly clamorous, and it was evident that if I did not quickly petition my beauty, the field would be left open to my rivals by my removal to the King's Bench. In this dilemma, I wrote to my father, explaining my speculations, and humbly confessing my present difficulties: in reply, I received a hearty congratulation, and a draft on his banker for £500, which the generous old gentleman hoped would not only cover all my debts, but enable me to sport a little in pursuit of the widow; he little thought that his remittance would be as a mere drop in the ocean of my debts. It certainly quieted the clamours of my creditors for a time, and enabled me to run up a longer score of credit on the strength of a little more display: but the shallowness of my resources was soon discovered; and at last, in order to avoid the interior of a sponging-house, I saw it was positively necessary to win my beautiful enslaver, and her twenty-five thousand, at once, or give leg-bail to my creditors; and although I felt everything but confident of the issue, I determined to try my fortune at once.

The day that was to decide my fate was ushered in with one of those dense yellow fogs, the atmosphere of link-boys, and the bane of gas-contractors; a fog in which a spoon would stand upright, and in breathing which a hungry man may fancy that he is swallowing a hearty mess of smoked pea-soup. The weather alone was sufficient to damp a man's ardour, and I was sadly inclined to look upon the dark side of my undertaking.

As I approached Cavendish Square, my heart rose to my mouth, and I could not help foreboding that all my lofty castles were destined that day to be dashed to the ground. The streets were greasy and slippery, and in turning the corner of Holles Street, my foot slipped off the rounded edge of the pavement, and down I came plump in the mud. Here was a pickle for a lover going in form to pop the awful question; besides, this was my only Stultz fit to wear. I was fully convinced that my evil star presided that day, and having got a wipe-down at Bull and Churton's, I determined to postpone my visit until the morrow. I turned back, and on arrival at my lodgings, found the door surrounded by a multitude of tradesmen and duns, rendering it necessary that I should avoid placing my person in their vicinity, if I wished to continue at large. I therefore turned off in the direction of Belgrave Square, with a resolution to explain my uncomfortable position to my friend Lady A., and to beg her advice and assistance.

It was in no very enviable mood that I arrived at Belgrave

Square, and gave an angry summons to the porter. I was admitted, and hastened upstairs, unannounced, being told that her ladyship was alone. At the drawing-room door, however, I made a sudden halt, for to my utter astonishment, a man's voice, in loud and passionate entreaty, was audible within. I turned into the adjoining room to await the lady's leisure, having despatched a servant for another suit of raiment; here, however, I found that in consequence of the folding doors, every word spoken in the next room was plainly heard, and on this account I was about to shift my quarters, when I caught a few words from a voice never to be mistaken by me, and which instantly awakened all the evil passions of my soul—jealousy and revenge were uppermost, and I advanced to the door for the purpose of interrupting the *tête-à-tête*, when my attention was fixed by what was passing within.

'Now oblige me by rising,' said the lady; 'I cannot suffer you to continue in that attitude; we shall be interrupted presently. Get up, sir; I tell you I will not answer your question.'

'Dearest Mrs Monk, tell me, is it Howard? Remember, he must soon be returning to India; surely you would never think of burying those angelic charms in a land of cholera and cobra-de-capellas; you would not squander that exquisite refinement and finish upon the demi-barbarous society of those pestilential climes: only tell me if it be he, that I may fly to destroy him for his infamous presumption!'

'I tell, you, sir, I will answer you no question. By what right, sir, do you dare to catechize me? You had better get up now; I am growing seriously angry, and will positively cut off this fine treasured whisker if you do not rise.' The threat appeared to take effect.

'And now, Mr Brown,' cried the lady, 'I shall feel obliged if you will take your leave. Let me once more assure you that your addresses are an annoyance to me, much as you flatter me. Now, sir, depart, I pray you, or I shall not keep civil terms with you much longer.'

'But, my dear madam, you asked me what I had to offer in return for your lovely person and the £25,000. I do solemnly assure you I had not the remotest idea that you had still so large a fortune; I had heard rumours that you had liberally spent or given away the greater part of your estate. You must be well aware, madam, that avarice forms no part of my character.'

'Indeed, Mr Brown, I cannot and will not be detained with a recital of your good or bad qualities. I am alike indifferent to both. If you do not take your leave forthwith, I shall be apt to consider you unworthy of the delicacy with which I have hitherto treated you.'

'Nay, now, peace, I pray you. If I could but convince you of my devotion—surely if poverty be an objection, it must apply equally to Howard as to myself. The pay of a captain in the Indian army is but a bare pittance: besides. I have heard it whispered that Howard is no captain after all, but that he holds the exalted rank of ensign in a regiment of Native Infantry, upon a salary of about a hundred a year.'

'But, sir, I can assure you, that Howard is a captain. I met a friend of his, a major in his corps, who assured me that he was what they call a *pucka* captain, that is, without brevet rank, and holding a company, which is more fortunate promotion than falls to the lot of every young man in the army in these days: his pay, I am told, is in excess of £600 a year. This I only mention in justice to Captain Howard, and not because I have any interest in him beyond that of a passing acquaintance.'

'You have said enough, madam: the warmth of your manner tells me who is my rival. Adieu! madam; trust me you shall shortly hear of your slave, Captain Howard.'

Brown made his exit at the staircase door as I slipped in at the other. The lady's back was towards me, and as I entered, noiselessly, she did not turn, or appear to be aware of my presence. For an instant I thought that I caught a glance of her eye in the opposite mirror, but I again fancied that I must have been mistaken, when I heard a deep sigh from the fair one, and 'Poor Howard! I fear I have treated him very capriciously; I wish he would call,'—uttered in a scarcely audible voice. In a moment I was at her feet— popped—and was accepted. I begged for a speedy solemnization; my beauty said a month; but I pleaded hard, and a week from that day was ultimately fixed upon. Pretty sharp work, certainly; but we had mutually an utter contempt of anything slow.

Although I swore that I was perfectly indifferent to anything like money matters in the business, still the lady insisted upon it that her attorney should explain to me the position of her affairs; and truly the little man showed me a power of parchment, and a balance sheet of some £30,000 on the right side; the documents of the £25,000 being too clear to be misunderstood. Mr Murphy agreed to silence my creditors for me, although he was sorry that he could only supply them with promises at present, as it would be an incalculable loss to touch even a fraction of Mrs M.'s fortune just at the present moment; the whole of it being embarked in speculations, upon which it would entail positive ruin if a six-pence were withdrawn. Of course I did not care, as long as they were silent, whether my creditors were paid in cash or promises.

The wedding was to be very quiet, at the request of the lady, a stipulation to which I was unwillingly compelled to accede. Lady A. and a very few of our more immediate intimates, were alone to be present at the ceremony. All preliminaries had been comfortably arranged, and on the critical morning I went to Cavendish Square in a handsome job chariot, at nine o'clock. On entering the breakfast parlour I was politely and cheerfully greeted by Murphy the attorney with a shower of congratulations; and while listening to the little man's encomiums most lavishly bestowed upon my charming, and amiable, and accomplished, and beautiful, and brilliant, and fascinating bride, the lady herself entered, most tastefully arrayed in a bridal robe of white satin, trimmed with blond. Though paler than usual, she was more lovely than ever, and I involuntarily said in, my heart, 'Happy dog should I be even without the twenty-five thousand.'

'Ah! my Howard', said she, 'you look handsomer than ever. Stay; that left moustache—that will do. Dear Lady A. has a wretched side-ache this morning, and is unable to leave her chamber. How very provoking that I should be deprived of her kind support on such an occasion as this! However, we will allow nothing to damp our spirits today. The two Misses Anderson have also sent excuses for themselves and their mamma; they have this moment received tidings of the death of a near relation, and of course we could not expect them; though I think they might have sealed up the letter again, and have allowed it to remain upon the mantelpiece until the evening. This is really unfortunate; but never mind, my Howard, we will be all in all to one another.'

'Yes, my sweet. Mr Murphy then will be the only friend present at the wedding?'

'Why, yes, love, and must give me away. It is very annoying to be thus disappointed by all our friends, but we shall be just as well married without them. James, you know, can be second witness.'

After the celebration of our nuptials, all went on as happily as heart could wish, for the first few weeks. My creditors had for a time lost sight of me, but I was again scented out; duns followed upon duns; promises would go no further. I determined, therefore, to apply to my devoted wife, who I knew would refuse me nothing, and to explain to her the extremity of my situation. I seized a handful of bills, and ascending to her dressing-room, I entered with as unconcerned a brow as possible, thinking it best to make light of the matter at first.

Mrs H. was sitting before the cheval glass in—but I will not introduce you into her sanctum. An amiable honeymoon smile greeted me on my entrance; but the expression of her face changed, as she caught a glimpse of the red lines and figures of the papers I held in my hand.

'Now, Howard, why do you enter my room without knocking? Really this visit is very unseasonable; oblige me by leaving the room.'

'Why, my pretty one, what is the matter? You never chid me before; and I have been in your dressing-room a hundred times without knocking.'

'I tell you, I won't permit it. I beg you will leave me!'

'Certainly, my love; but as I am here, I may as well mention what I came for; here is—'

'Captain Howard, did you understand me? Do you mean to go, sir, or must I return to my bedroom? How do you know my—'

'Well, my sweet girl, don't be angry; I'm off!'

Mrs Howard, it appeared, was too much indisposed to come down to breakfast this morning, so I carried some upstairs to her myself, and with a gentle tap at the door, 'My love, may I come in?'

'Not just now, my dear Howard. What do you want?'

'I have brought you up some breakfast.'

'Thank you, love; Smith will take it of you; but I cannot see you just now.'

Foiled again, I saw that I must await the lady's pleasure, as all good husbands should. In the course of the morning, however, Mrs H. made her appearance, all smiles and good humour, much to my relief. 'Well, my Charles,' said she, 'what did you want? It was very naughty of you to enter my room without knocking; but of course you did not know— I'm sorry I spoke so cross to you, love; what did you want?'

'Oh, nothing, my sweet girl, I thank you; only I have been dunned by these infernal creditors till I'm almost mad. However, it's not much, my love; it won't put you to any inconvenience: here is a bill for three fifties, and there are half a dozen others for about the same amount, some less, some more, which I know you will readily—'

'Oh, don't mention it, my love; certainly Murphy must supply you with whatever is necessary.'

'My love, Murphy declares he cannot, at any sacrifice, touch a single six-pence of your money until the next commercial year, as it is all involved in speculations, from which he cannot withdraw any portion of it. To tell you the truth, I am suspicious of that man; he is too obsequious and cringing to be trusted, and yet you appear to know nothing at all about your own money matters. Promises won't do any longer; cash I must have, to stop the hands of these insatiate jackals, or I shall be walked off to the King's Bench before I am twelve hours older. Why, at this moment, the door is surrounded by a whole host of these vile harpies, who vow either to have payment of their claims, or to execute the writs with which they are furnished. Now, madam, you must either come down with the cash at once, or I must make your jewels and *bijouterie* answer my purpose until cash can be got on loan or mortgage.'

'But, my love, Murphy has written—'

'Murphy be —'

'Well, Howard, it appears then that the game is up, and the best thing we can do now is to get clear out of this as quickly as possible; and as the demands against you seem to be serious, we had better be off to India at once.'

'India! what with £30,000 in the treasury? Thank ye, Mrs Howard; but you're joking, surely. Come now, talk sense; let me set some respectable man at work to see what Murphy is doing with all this money; and then these paltry debts of mine can be discharged, and we may live comfortably enough upon the property if we sink it. Why, the whole of my debts don't amount to more than £3,000 or £5,000.'

'Well, I see how it is, Howard; and, as I said before, the game is now fairly up—I may as well say it plainly—I have not a penny in the world.'

'Fire and furies, Mrs Howard. Then what the devil were those parchments which I saw? Nay, now, you are joking with me.'

'No, Howard, what I have said is too true. I had £25,000, and have gambled and squandered away not only all of that, but £6,000 more, to which amount I am now in debt, without a hope of liquidation.'

'Well, curse your impudence. But, tell me, madam, what, in the name of all that is ridiculous, could have induced you to bestow yourself upon a poor penniless wretch like me?'

'Why, you know, my dear, that your rank of captain in

the Bengal army, and your pay, some five or six hundred a
year, will always keep me respectable, which I fear would
hardly have been the case had I been left much longer upon
my own resources.'

'Ha! ha! ha! Captain! Five or six hundred a year!!
Excellent!!! Well, thank God, I am even with you there. Why,
my darling, I am third ensign of my regiment; and as for the
five or six hundred, I ought to have certainly about a hundred
and seventy; but unfortunately one-half of it is forestalled by
the Military Court of Requests, for the benefit of my creditors
in India.'

An eloquent pause—

'Howard, resumed the lady, 'We are both fairly punished.
No reproaches, now; you see how matters stand; now do you
not agree with me, that the wisest thing to be done is to
forget, if possible, this unfortunate marriage? It would be
childish to quarrel, but let us part forthwith; I will find
means of quitting London, and probably England too. You
had better be off to India as speedily as possible. Eh? what
say you?'

'With all my heart, my lovely one; now you are really a
sensible woman: I will but send for my dear friend Murphy,
and pay him the balance in his favour. I'm not angry with
you, love, but I must wipe off all scores with that hypocrite
Murphy; my other debts must stand over.'

'You can't pay him, Howard; here is his P.P.C.'

'My dear Madam:

'We are blown beyond redemption; so I have only
time to give you warning to quit town as precipitately
as I have done. Many thanks for past favours.

Yours ever obediently,
Humphrey Murphy

'So, then fare you well, my love. One kiss; there, 'tis a pretty thing, and I pity it. Good bye.'

I made my exit by the fire-escape, and walked over ten or twelve houses before I could find a door open.' I was a stranger to the inhabitants, but I determined to risk a passage, and entered. On the second floor I met a servant, who was not a little surprised at falling in with a visitor from the garrets; and doubtless he would have disputed my further progress, had not his hands been fortunately well occupied in bearing a weighty tiffin tray, loaded with sundry smoking viands and a fit concomitant of bottles and glassware. At first I thought of passing him at a long trot; but I had much to fear from an alarm, and therefore thought it more expedient to inquire for the master of the house, and beg an interview. The fellow looked very suspiciously at me, and returning to the head of the stairs, he called out, "Ere, John, lend a heye 'ere a moment, while I lets master know as this gentleman wants a hinterview.'

The knight of the napkin carried his tray into a room whence proceeded the grumbling of certain voices, while John kept a sharp look-out upon me from the landing-place. in a moment, out came a jolly looking old gentleman, with a rubicund face as round as the crown of your hat, a Bardolphian gnomon in the centre, and in the corner of his mouth the latter end of an Havannah cigar. 'Well, who the deuce are you, sir? How came ye up in my maids' berths, and what were ye doing there?'

I made a brief explanation of my situation with regard to my creditors, and begged that he would permit me to make his house a thoroughfare, as my only chance of avoiding their pursuit.

'Howard? Howard? Don't know the name, sir; No. 38.

Excuse me, my good sir, but one's obliged to be particular in London. Here, John, step over to No. 38; inquire the name, and just see if there are any sharks in the wake. Mr Howard, walk in; and as soon as the lad returns, you shall be at liberty. These gentlemen, sir, are brother commodores of mine; pray be seated. I'm sorry you should find me in such a hurry-scurry, but I'm just going to sea, and have broken up housekeeping.' Further conversation elicited that the worthy gentleman into whose company I was thus accidentally thrown, was commander of a merchant ship outward-bound for Calcutta, with one vacant cabin. We came to terms. and here I am.

The Faithless Fiancé

British women took the voyage to India either to join their husbands there or to find husbands for themselves. Unmarried women travelled usually under the care of chaperones. If alone, they were placed under the charge of the ship's captain. Parents would instruct their daughters on how to deport themselves and to avoid romantic entanglements during the long voyage. The presence of a few young women on board a shipload of men naturally led to the men competing for their favours. Many a romance on board ended in happy union. In their passionate involvement some of them even ignored their earlier engagements or commitments and got themselves married before they landed in India.

The following episode is drawn from Mrs Major Clemons's book Manners and Customs of Society in India *(1841).*

Henry C——, an exceedingly handsome youth, about eighteen years old, joined the army at Hyderabad as cadet in 1822. He was much admired by all at the station, and truly beloved by many; his manners were winning, and his disposition most amiable. He had become attached to a young, lady about his own age before he quitted England; but the want of fortune on both sides prevented his bringing her to India as his wife; the youth of the parties was also made an objection by her parents. They promised to be faithful to each other, and agreed, that as soon as he was a Lieutenant, and could save a sufficient sum of money, he should send it home to pay for her passage out. Time passed; they continued to correspond, and her picture, which he had brought to India with him, was frequently looked at, and regarded by him as the greatest consolation.

In 1828 he was promoted as Lieutenant, and then did he anticipate the realization of all his dreams of happiness. He denied himself nearly every comfort, in order to save his pay; he had previously put a little away monthly out of his ensign's allowance, and now he doubled it, and in the course of a year he had realized the wished-for sum. One hundred pounds were remitted to England, while he still continued his economical mode of living, that he might have a small store of money to commence house-keeping when she should arrive in India. His very life seemed wrapped up in her. He would frequently talk to his friends about her, show them her picture, and expatiate on her accomplishments—her affectionate letters—her truth and constancy of attachment.

At last the much-wished-for letter arrived which was the answer to his own. She was coming—had sailed—might be expected in four short weeks. Then was the bustle of preparation, a pretty bungalow was taken, neatly furnished with everything of comfort, and even elegance. She was to come to his friend's house from the ship, and take up her abode there, till she was carried as a bride to her own residence. Morning and evening did Lieutinant C—— gallop down to the beach, expecting the long desired vessel to appear in sight. At last an English ship was signaled—the very ship that contained all that was dear to him.

The list of passengers had been sent on shore, before the

ship came to anchor, according to the general custom. His anxious eyes ran over it; but no Miss—— was there. What could this mean? His mind was harassed with a thousand speculations. She must be dead—have fallen overboard—been left ill at the Cape, or at Madeira? What could it be?—But he would wait till the letters were ready for delivery; he would certainly get a letter, and then he would know the worst. He paced the beach full of anxiety, and called every ten minutes to know if the letters were ready.

At last the time arrived, and all were getting welcome communications, from parents, brothers, friends—delightful intelligence from the dear and distant home. None can describe the delight of such moments but those who have been for years in a foreign land, separated from all the dear objects of youth, those who still hold with freshness the memory of past days, who feel that neither time nor change of circumstances have lessened the heart's warm glow. It is in those moments that they forget that seas divide them, and that they may never in this world meet again.

But to return. There was no letter for Lieutenant C——! He was now unable to guess at the probabilities of silence. If she had been ill she would undoubtedly have written, or caused some other person to have done so. Hope again came to his distracted mind. The captain of the ship, under whose charge she was to leave England, might have a letter. He, therefore, went to the agents of the ship, as most probably the captain would first go to them; and waited with as much patience as his agitation would permit. The gentleman came. 'You are the captain of the ship just anchored, the ——, I am Lieutenant C—— of the —— regiment, and expected a young lady, Miss—— to have sailed with you from London. As I find she is not in the list of your passengers, perhaps you may have a letter for me?'

'Indeed, Lieutenant C——,' replied the captain, 'I have no letter for you; but I have a communication to make, which I trust you will bear with becoming fortitude, and I should think, and hope, that when you have heard the whole, your regret will almost be turned to rejoicing.'

'What can you mean?—She must be dead!—and would that be a cause of rejoicing to me, captain? I cannot bear this suspense:tell me all, at once.'

'My dear Mr C——, I am really sorry that I am obliged to be the bearer of a tale, that, in any way, must be a heavy blow to you, and perhaps it will be best that I should be as brief as possible. Miss —— sailed with me from London: her father placed her under my protection for the voyage; but you must be well aware that her age was such as to prevent me having an entire control over her. My ship was full of passengers, amongst whom was Captain N——. We had not been more than a month at sea, when a great intimacy was formed between Miss —— and that gentleman. They were always together on deck, and when the, weather prevented them being there, letters constantly passed between the cabins. I am a father and a husband, sir, and I ventured to mention to her the impropriety of her conduct in allowing an officer to pay his addresses to her, while she was positively engaged to another. She was pleased to say that she was sensible of my kindness; but that since she had seen Captain N——, she found she could never fulfil her engagement with Lieutenant C——: it would be wrong in her to plight her faith to him at the altar, when her heart was now wholly another's. I could say no more; but after this, Miss —— kept her cabin more closely than she had done before; perhaps she shrunk from my reproving eye. In nine weeks we reached the Cape, where we remained five days. Need I say that Miss ——

came on board again as Mrs N——. Sincerely do I sympathize with you in your natural feelings; but consider, my dear sir, how highly probable it is, that a young lady of this description would, even after your marriage with her, have never returned that warm affection so necessary to the wedded life; therefore I again say, you must rejoice, and not grieve for your loss.'

It is needless to say how deeply poor C—— felt this blow. He lay on the couch, weeping bitterly; it was well that his feelings could thus give themselves vent. He suffered much, and long; but the kindness of his brother officers at length soothed his grief, and the regiment being about to march, he was aroused for a time from the state of despondency into which he was fast sinking. He never regained his former spirits, and his general health had evidently sustained a severe shock. He lived but two years after this disappointment, and, strange to say, Mrs N—— survived him but two months. They never met, as Captain N—— was at a station some two or three hundred miles away.

The Hollow Tooth

*The Indian marriage market attracted many British women in the
early nineteenth century when they came to shop for husbands
from among the John Company's bachelor officials. There were
promising prospects not only for the young and blooming but also
the spinsters. Marriage proposals, brisk and unsentimental, came
in abundance, requiring them to make quick decisions about rival
suitors. Many alliances were concluded in haste since opportunities
for meeting or ascertaining the character and family background of
prospective bridegrooms were virtually non-existent. The
consequences of such unions were often disastrous. Coming from a
situation of mediocrity with gloomy prospects of marriage at home,
many of these women after wedlock suddenly found themselves in
a state of opulence and luxury, but burdened with partners totally
incompatible with their nature and temperament. The frivolous
ones made themselves bold and looked for amours outside the
wedlock.*

*This tale of the escapades of a young memsahib caught in an
ill-matched union is taken from the* Lays of Ind *by Aliph Cheem.*

Mr Commissioner icey chill
Possessed a youthful wife,
An unbending neck, an inflexible will,
And gloomy views of life.

The height of his pleasure consisted in
Denouncing smiles and jokes,
And groaning and moaning over sin,
Especially other folks'.

He sat one day in his office seat,
With a frown upon his face;
And at eventide, when he came to eat,
He sighed as he said the grace.

For hadn't his Ruth, so frivolous been
To the recent bachelor's ball,
In spite of his saying a ball was a scene
He couldn't approve at all?

And hadn't a Mr Harvey Sauce
Called twice in the self-same week?
And wasn't it shocking? It was, of course
And wasn't he right to speak?

For didn't all bachelor army men
Lead highly immoral lives?
And didn't they every now and then
Steal other people's wives?

And hadn't he many a time with force
Explained all this to Ruth?
And hadn't she said that Mr Sauce
Was quite an exceptional youth.

A gentleman quite, from tip to top,
And as innocent as a mouse?
And hadn't he thought it wise to stop
His frisking about the house?

And hadn't he her severely chid,
And wasn't she underhand,
Talking away—yes, that she did—
To the rascal at the Band?

And hadn't he laid before her bare
The wickedness of her life,
And very solemnly told her where
Her duty lay as a wife?

And didn't he say that her pranks must end,
And her gadding about; but he
Would allow her to ask a serious friend
Or a clergyman, in to tea?

And that, lest she'd be dull, he wished her soon
To make a regular rule
Of teaching every afternoon
In the neighbouring Mission school?

And didn't she fume and chafe and fret
When he ventured thus to speak,
And work herself into an obstinate pet,
Which lasted the rest of the week?

And didn't he patiently bear with her still,
Reading her sermons nice,
And praying aloud that her evil will
Might yield to his good advice?

And didn't he even show her how
That hers was a fortunate lot?
And wasn't there then an awful row?
And didn't he catch it hot?

And now he ate his dinner alone—
For Ruth avoided the room—
He sighed as he picked his chicken bone,
And his face was full of gloom.

For he couldn't and wouldn't to her give in,
Nor compromise with wrong;
And he meant to be firm this time, and win,
Though the struggle might be long.

❧

It was; but woman, you know, is weak,
And abhors protracted strife.
Ruth suddenly seemed to grow quite meek,
And to change the way of her life.

No Harvey Sauce to be seen by her trap
In the evening at the Band;
No novel at midday in her lap;
No scented chit in her hand.

Propriety reigned in the bungalow
From morning unto night,
And she didn't appear to find it slow,
Though she very justly might.

Thought Chill to himself, 'My duty's done—
I've plucked out sin by the roots,'
And over the victory that he'd won
He rose an inch in his boots.

So time wore on, and exempt from blame,
And quite at her ease seemed Ruth,
Till a cloud of trouble and sorrow came
In the shape of a hollow tooth.

❧

It was white as a pearl; not cankered a bit;
Just like the rest of her teeth;
But it pained, and the doctor who looked at it
Said the hollow was underneath.

For a month she wriggled and writhed and groaned
With a flannel bag at her cheek,
And Icey Chill was frightened, and owned
That she seemed to be getting weak.

Then a couple of learned doctors met,
And, after debate and doubt,
They told the husband, with great regret,
They dreaded to pull it out.

'T was a ticklish case of internal decay;
Quite out of their line, they felt;
And the only thing was to go to Bombay,
Where a regular dentist dwelt.

Then Icey Chill emitted a groan,
And dried a tear with his sleeve,
For his darling would have to travel alone,
As 'he wasn't entitled to leave.'

And his precious darling, she didn't lag,
She started without delay,
With her head tied up in a flannel bag,
On her journey to Bombay.

The sufferer travelled as fast as she could,
And arrived in proper course;
And on the platform a dentist stood
Of the name of Harvey Sauce!

❧

It was terrible work when Icey Chill
Discovered the ugly truth;
And even now he will turn quite ill
If you speak of a hollow tooth.

And time has failed to remove the sting,
Though damages and divorce
Made dentistry rather a costly thing
For Mr Harvey Sauce.

He had to borrow, and then to sell,
Then went to the bottom, flop
And Ruth—of course she merits it well—
Is making shirts for a shop.

In fact, the moralists, stem of heart,
Herein may find relief;
Both played an extremely shady part,
And properly came to grief.

And what of Icey, the victim?—alas!
The good of suffer in life;
And a gloomy man is a terrible ass
To marry a frivolous wife.

Infatuation in Middle Age

Until the beginning of the nineteenth century, the number of young marriageable European girls was so small that they could easily pick and choose their husbands in the Indian marriage bazaar. Among those who chose to marry older men with rank and wealth, there were some who later on could not resist the temptation of yielding to the advances of young gallants, especially when they discovered their husbands indulging in extralmarital flings. Eliza Draper's was one such case. She could not keep her virtuous resolutions when she found her husband having an affair with the housekeeper. Overwhelmed by her admirers' compliments she became the chief attraction at Government House balls and was besieged by young men pining to have a dance with her. Finally she found compensation in the loving arms of a naval officer. After her elopement with him from Belvedere House in Bombay she went to live in London. But stories abounded about her ghost which was said to haunt the place.

Her story is taken from British Social Life in India, 1608-1937 *by Dennis Kincaid (1938).*

Eliza was born in 1744 at Anjengo, in Malabar, where her father was employed in the English store. A district of jungles and mudflats and endless creeks; a village of thatched cottages hidden among tall palms that hissed and swayed in the warm damp wind. There was no school here for Eliza and one can only suppose that it was from her parents that she learnt her varied accomplishments. She was ugly, and yet even as a child there is evidence of her extraordinary charms. The tree under which she used to rest after her evening stroll along the beach was known for a century as 'Eliza's Tree'. The Abbé Raynal who met her long afterwards in Bombay wrote ecstatically of her fascination. 'Anjengo,' he exclaimed, 'you are nothing but you have given birth to Eliza!' and the Abbé knew all the most accomplished women in Paris in the great age of conversation, wit and charm. And James Forbes, a renowned Company civil servant famous for his *Oriental Memoirs* who so seldom praised without qualification, admitted with a sigh that a description of her attraction was beyond his powers. 'Her refined tastes and elegant accomplishments need no encomium from my pen.' But in Anjengo there were few to admire her and she must have been grateful to Mr Daniel Draper who, on a visit from Bombay, proposed to her. Gloomy, pompous and twenty years older than Eliza, he must nevertheless have seemed a most desirable husband both to Eliza and her parents, for he was a great man in Bombay, Secretary to Government and already spoken of as destined to the highest posts. She was happy with him at first and when, some years later, he suggested a visit to England she was enraptured. On the ship were two Bombay friends, Commodore and Mrs James. The Commodore was something of a hero, for he had attacked and broken the power of Angria; while his wife was a woman of culture with many friends in literary London. Among them was Lawrence Sterne, and she enjoyed 'the almost unique distinction of being the only woman outside his own family circle whom Sterne never approached in the language of artificial gallantry, but always in that of simple friendship and respect'. Soon after they arrived in London, Mrs James gave a dinner party and among the guests were the Drapers and Sterne. Sterne fell instantly and desperately in love with the ugly but fascinating girl from India, and she was swept off her feet by his tempestuous and tragic style of wooing (so different from Daniel's formal expressions of affection). He affected to believe her still unmarried and would write—

Pray, Eliza, do not think of giving yourself to some wealthy nabob, because I design to marry you myself. My wife cannot live long—she has sold all the provinces of France already. And I know not the woman I should like so well for her substitute as yourself. 'Tis true I am ninety-five in constitution and you but twenty-five—rather too great a disparity this?—but what I want in youth I will make up in wit and good humour. Not Swift so loved his Stella, Scarron his Maintenon, or Waller his Sacharina as I will love thee and sing thee, my wife elect.

Eliza who knew nothing of Sterne's life believed all this rigmarole. 'I believed Sterne,' she cried, 'simplicity I believed him; I had no motive to do otherwise than believe him just, generous and unhappy.' In the letters they exchanged she called him 'mild, generous and good youth' and he called her his 'Bramine'. But when Mr Draper's leave came to an end Eliza had to follow her husband back to Bombay. Sterne's letters became increasingly hysterical. 'Eliza, from the highest Heaven, my first and last country, receive my oath; I swear not to write one line in which my friend may not be recognized.' They were not destined to meet again, for soon after Eliza's return Sterne 'was taken ill at the silk-bag shop in Old Bond Street'; he was carried home to his lodgings and there 'put up his hand as if to stop a blow and died in a minute'. Mrs Sterne and her daughter, finding some copies of Sterne's letters to Eliza, tried to blackmail her with the threat of publication. Eliza wrote in alarm from Bombay to Mrs James. 'To add to my regret for his loss, his widow has my letters in her power (I never entertained a good opinion of her) and means to subject me to disgrace and inconvenience by the publication of them.' Although this threat never materialized, the rumour of Eliza's correspondence with an eminent man of letters had, as Eliza complained, 'somehow become extremely public at this settlement' and in her constant alarm lest the rumour should reach Daniel's ears she must have been very grateful for his sudden transfer from Bombay to Tellichery where he had been appointed chief of the factory. She was happy in this new station and tried to forget the past. She began to interest herself in her husband's work and even worked as his amanuensis. She enjoyed her new importance as wife of the head of the factory, she was flattered by the deference of the Indian employees and merchants, and in her letters she extolled their superior culture, describing the place as the 'Montpellier of India'. She wrote that

> the Country is pleasant and healthy ... our house a Magnificent one, furnished too at our Master's expense and the allowance for supporting it Creditably what you would term Genteely, tho' it does not defray the charge of our Liquors which alone amount to six hundred a year ... Our Society at other times is very confined as it only consists of a few Factors and two or three Families; and such we cannot expect great intercourse with, on account of

the heavy rains and terrible thunder and lightning to which this coast is peculiarly subject six months in the year. 'Tis call'd that of Malabar ... Mahé is not more than seven Miles Distant from us (Yet very few civilities pass between us and the Monsieurs) and Cochin (a Sweet Spot) about two days' Sail.

Unfortunately for Eliza's virtuous resolutions Daniel received a new promotion and was recalled to Bombay and appointed Member of Council. Once more Eliza attracted admiration and when she appeared at balls at Government House in hoop and farthingale factors and cadets besieged her for dances. There was not, of course, much competition; there were only thirty-nine ladies in the station, thirty-three of them married, five widows and one, 'Winnifred Daires, Unmarried Woman' as she was somewhat ungallantly described on an invitation list. The Governor was then Hornby, and his interest in magic and the fact that he was 'ignorant not only of the first principles of Government, but of the ordinary knowledge requisite for a gentleman' did not prevent him from giving a series of successful balls at which Eliza was always the chief attraction. The Drapers now lived in a house at Mazagon, called Belvedere, a long yellow building, formerly a Portuguese convent, on a mound overlooking the sea and pleasantly shaded by palms. Cadets and factors would walk along the sands in the mornings to call on the Drapers (morning calls were then fashionable), and would sit and talk in the airy drawing-room. They were probably very cheerful, for the first morning visit of almost every cadet was to some other cadet's quarters where he would be welcomed with draughts of punch and of 'arrack and water, which, however cool and pleasant at the moment was succeeded by the most deleterious effects'. Then, sufficiently refreshed, they would set out on their calls, not without some jeers at the few virtuous youths 'who devoted their morning hours to music, drawing, literary improvement and other rational pursuits'. Probably the visits and compliments of the young factors and cadets would have kept Eliza amused without involving her in any serious entanglement, but for the sudden interest that the severe and frigid Daniel began to take in the housekeeper, Mrs Leeds. Eliza noticed that when he went to his bedroom for his afternoon siesta, he used to call for Mrs Leeds to help him put on the 'Conjee cap' that he wore in place of his wig when resting. It always appeared to take Mrs Leeds a long time to help him with his cap and Eliza had to protest against 'your avowed preference for Leeds to myself', but Daniel paid no attention. It is difficult to blame Eliza for finding compensation in the ardent suit of a naval officer called Clark; and when Daniel's middle-aged infatuation for Mrs Leeds made life at Belvedere intolerable for Eliza, she let herself down by a rope from her bedroom window and took refuge on Clark's ship, leaving behind a pathetic note for her husband, 'I go. I know not whither, but I will never be a tax on you, Draper. I am not a hardened or depraved creature. The enclosed are the only bills that I know of, except six rupees to Doojee, the shoemaker.' She was received with enthusiasm in literary circles in London and now, no longer troubled by scruples over their effect on Mr Draper, authorized the publication of Sterne's letters to her. She died in 1778 and was buried at Bristol. The epitaph on her tomb, 'In her Genius and Benevolence were united', is a curious constrast to that on the gravestone of Sterne, 'Ah! *Molliter ossa quiescant.*' Daniel, having become President of the Bombay Council, retired in great affluence and lived very virtuously in St James's Street where no one had heard of Mrs Leeds.

A Marriage Made in Heaven

Many British soldiers of the East India Company's army were stationed in places far away from the Presidency towns of Calcutta, Bombay and Madras. Lacking female company and other means of amusement, they led a dull, solitary existence made even more difficult by the rigours of climate and exposure to sickness. Coming to India young and for the most part devoted to pleasure or hungry for gain and without any religious influence, they changed in strange ways. Some took to shawls and turbans, others frequented sacred river ghats or bathing places and a few of them even came under the spell of Hindu mendicants and began believing in supernatural communication through dreams and visions.

This story is taken from Lt. Thomas Bacon's memoirs, First Impressions and Studies from Nature in Hindostan *(1837).*

Major Vangricken was a fine old soldier who had lost his leg at Aracan. A man of gigantic stature and great bodily prowess, he had features which were small, but regular; and his restless eye, significant of talent and acute inquisitiveness, bore also an expression of irritation, fully accounted for by the vague subjects of his conversation. His mental infirmity was easily discovered, but not without the exhibition of a strong though warped imagination, and the pitiable wreck of what had once been a well adorned and vigorous mind. His conversation emitted sparks of an original and vivid genius, and in every discussion he managed to amuse his listeners no less than he surprised them: he possessed that unaccountable, though by no means rare combination, of puerile simplicity in some things, with brilliant conception in others, together with powerful energy of inference and argument, so surprising in many instances of insanity. The wildest speculations and most visionary schemes were grasped at by him with an avidity truly ludicrous: but then they were supported by a wonderfully plausible and imposing eloquence, which it required a close and mature investigation to expose. His favourite subjects were those of scientific and mechanical inventions, which during his furlough he had laboured to advance at the sacrifice of his health and his means, without even the advantage of discovering the vanity of his impracticable design. Had he lived during the reign of alchemy he would assuredly have plunged head and ears into the occult science, for he still believed in the existence of the elixir vitae, and would have enlisted in the pursuit had he deemed any one human life of sufficient endurance to allow a hope of success.

There was one speculation upon which he had built his hopes of immortal fame, and which everlastingly engrossed his speculative ingenuity; this all-absorbing project was no other than the practicability of adapting wings to the human body. He firmly believed in the possibility of the design, and had dissipated a considerable sum of money in London in endeavouring to realize this chimera. Another of his themes, infinitely more absurd, was the idea of training the larger tribes of the winged creation to the humility of taking a rider on their backs, to be governed like a horse, by bit and bridle; or to the more complete degradation of submitting to become birds of burden, for the transportation of posts and packets.

It is not improbable that these strange devices took root in his diseased imagination during his illness in Aracan, when his mind was possibly bent upon a return to his native country; for even the plainest wishes of the heart become distorted pictures to the fevered brain of the suffering exile.

One day in Calcutta he had just risen from his bed, and was still in his nightly habiliments, when he was overcome with nervous excitement. His features were unusually swollen, and his eyes were red with watching through the greater part of the night. He sat at the foot of his couch, with his arms folded, his eyes fixed in abstraction, and the remnant of his mangled limb thrown out horizontally over the bedding, at an angle of forty-five from its more fortunate fellow. The moment he perceived Lt. Bacon who had called on him, his eye kindled with satisfaction, and, pointing to a chair, he begged him to listen while he related an account of a vision which had driven rest from his pillow, and which now engrossed his every thought.

Soon after he had retired to bed the previous night, he had been visited by an angel from heaven, bearing a special command that he, Vangricken, should repair to a certain commercial gentleman in Calcutta, and from him demand in marriage his only daughter, Miss Y., whom the heavenly messenger assured him should become the mother of a Saviour upon a new principle; one who should point out a new road to the celestial world, the old way being, he said, a little out of date, and in these days of reform considered somewhat roundabout. All this the poor maniac related to Lt. Bacon with the utmost gravity, and no small increase of consequence in his manner, on the score of the immense importance of the commission assigned to him.

He was evidently deeply and fearfully under the influence of the dream, and it would have been utter folly to have argued its absurdity, or in any way to have thwarted the inclination of his fancy. Bacon acquiesced in all his views upon the subject, but ventured to intimate that he should defer his visit to the gentleman until he should be favoured with some further development of the plan, and of the manner in which it should be accomplished. He regarded him suspiciously at first, but did not eventually object to delay the prosecution of the affair for at least a day or two; and when Bacon took his leave, he had the satisfaction of seeing him much more tranquil than when he had first entered.

A day or two afterwards, however, Bacon learnt that this composure had been all assumed, his suspicion having been aroused by his advice; he lost not a moment after his departure in repairing to Mr Y.'s office, for the purpose of entering upon the affair at once. On his arrival at the gentleman's establishment he was informed by a clerk that Mr Y. had not yet arrived, and would probably be found at his own house. Vangricken then enquired if the gentleman had a daughter.

'O yes, Sir,' replied the clerk.

'Is she pretty?' enquired the eager Vangricken.

'Really Sir, I am no judge in these matters, but I believe Miss Y. is accounted handsome by most people.'

'She is not black, eh?'

'Miss Y.?—no, indeed, Sir!'

'Ah, well, it's of no consequence—I will call upon Mr Y. I have just received the injunction of the Almightly to demand Miss Y. as a wife; so that you will excuse my having troubled you with these questions.'

Vangricken found Mr Y. and his daughter seated over the remnants of a late breakfast; and without any preamble, he entered at once upon the object of his visit. Mr Y. listened to him most attentively, and to the terror of his astonished daughter, betrayed neither surprise or indignation at this extraordinary overture. The madman watched with jealous scrutiny the effect of his proposal upon each of his auditors; the young lady was frightened almost into hysterics at the idea of the wooden leg, as she saw her father coolly deliberating upon the matter, as though he were really persuaded of its importance; at least, it was evident that he was by no means inclined to laugh at the proposal, or treat the visitor as a madman.

Poor girl! she became very seriously alarmed, and was about to quit the room, when her father spoke. 'Major Vangricken, this matter is truly one of paramount interest and extreme delicacy; now we must venture upon no conclusion without very mature deliberation. My love, do not leave the room; your presence will most probably be required. You will excuse me half a minute, my dear Sir, I have a note of some consequence to answer, and having got that off my mind, I shall be the better able to give my undivided attention to the subject in question.'

The note of consequence was quickly written, and dispatched to the general hospital, for half a dozen *he* fellows, accustomed to the charge of maniacs. As soon as the note had been sent off, Mr Y. entered fully upon the subject of his daughter's marriage, and they were just about to fix a day for the nuptials, when two European keepers, with a small train of able-bodied blacks, marched into the room, and impiously carried off the celestial bridegroom.

After this melancholy display of his malady, he was detained in confinement until the Medical Board thought fit to send him home again to England, there being no chance of his recovery under the maddening influence of a tropical climate.

The Compassionate Judge

Mr Justice Hyde was a highly respected figure in Calcutta during the late eighteenth century. Endowed with a sharp intellect and phenomenal memory, he was deeply influenced by moral and ethical considerations in dispensing justice. William Hickey, a leading attorney of Calcutta in those days, held Mr Hyde in high esteem for his kindness towards all those who had suffered at the hands of unscrupulous persons. In his fascinating memoirs which throw light on the life of the British community in Calcutta, Hickey narrates quite a few incidents to show the acts of benevolence of his favourite judge. The following episode, in Hickey's own words, is 'another proof of his (Hyde's) warmth of temper but equally so of his genuine sensibility'.

A man of the name of Sherif had acquired a handsome competence in the situation of an assistant extra clerk in the Calcutta treasury. This Mr Sherif debauched a young orphan girl, who thence-forward had cohabited with and been faithfully attached to her seducer, in the period of seven years bearing three children by him. At the end of that term he became enamoured of another woman who was obtainable only through wedlock. He therefore proposed to her, was accepted, and became a husband, upon which event he most ungenerously not only refused to make any provision for his

181

former favourite and mother of his children, but called upon the faithful and ill-used girl to give up a gold watch, with various other trinkets and ornaments of the person which he had presented to her at different times whilst she was residing with him. The poor creature's remonstrances against so illiberal and base a measure were unavailing. She therefore made a representation of her case in writing in the form of a petition, and delivered the same to Mr Justice Hyde, praying his lordship's interference to procure her redress and relief.

The humane judge felt keenly for her and was indignant at the vile conduct of her miserly betrayer; still he was conscious that the law did not authorize or warrant his compelling that betrayer to provide for the unhappy woman, or even make him restore the articles he so meanly took from her unless she could have established by witnesses that they had been actual gifts, which she candidly declared she could not do, having no such proofs within her power. Mr Hyde, however, resolved to try the effect of endeavouring to shame the man into an act of common justice, with which view he issued a summons in the usual form requiring Sherif to appear before him to answer a complaint made against him by the ill-treated woman, upon receiving which summons Sherif immediately took it to his lawyer to consult with him thereon, and having thus ascertained that the Judge could exercise no power over him upon the present occasion he went upon the day specified to the Judge's chambers, where Mr Hyde civilly told him the reason of his summoning him, expressing at the same time his hope that what was stated had been exaggerated, and that he could not have behaved so cruelly to an unprotected female.

Sherif, presuming upon what his lawyer had told him,

haughtily replied he did not consider himself bound to answer interrogatories, nor to reply to extra judicial questions. The latter phrase raised the Judge's choler, and he had, in consequence, recourse to his usual and favourite epithets of 'impertinent blockhead and stupid ass'. After a few seconds he thus addressed Sherif, 'Do you not think, sir, such conduct will deservedly render you contemptible in the eyes of every person of feeling, and an outcast from society?'

Sherif: 'No, I do not, nor do I see the least reason why it should have any such effect.'

Judge: 'Then you are wilfully blind and callous, for are you not a robber of the worst kind? Did you not plunder this poor destitute girl of the only patrimony she possessed, her chastity, and after so doing have you not basely and infamously abandoned her to want and misery, and yet you have the effrontery to say you are not unworthy the society of honest and honourable men!'

Sherif: 'I am the best judge of what is right to do and how to govern myself in matters which belong to me alone.'

Judge: 'I do not think so. You are upon the present occasion, and I lament that such is the case, beyond the reach of law. I possess not the power of compelling you to be commonly just, much less generous, but such grovelling, disgraceful sentiments as you have avowed must, I think, speedily bring you within the clutches of the law. I shall soon see you in a criminal court and will bear you in remembrance.'

Sherif: 'If to vent your scurrility is all you summoned me for I am not bound to wait for a continuance of it, nor will I.'

Judge: 'Oh, you won't! Then ere you depart let me ask you one question, which if you refuse to answer, I will answer for you. What are you, or what do you call yourself?'

Sherif: 'A gentleman!'

Judge: 'Oh! a gentleman. What, you wear shoes, I suppose! Every fellow that wears shoes in this country dubs himself gentleman. Got money, too, possibly, Mr Gentleman, a man of fortune?'

Sherif: 'Yes, I have ample fortune.'

Judge: 'How much may you be worth?'

Sherif: 'Upwards of two lacs of rupees!'

Judge: 'Upwards of two lacs of rupees, hey? And that you imagine constitues a gentleman? Why, you despicable wretch, an hundred lacs would not make you a gentleman, no wealth, no sum, no circumstances could do it. Go along. Get out, you contaminate the place. Take care of the approaching sessions. Get out, I say, vile wretch!'

Sherif seemed glad to obey the rough order and retired. The worthy Judge being thus foiled in his benevolent object, privately gave directions to his agent to pay the girl fifty sicca rupees every month without letting her know from what quarter it came, and to make the first payment that very day. This was actually done regularly for fifteen months; when the object of his bounty having discovered from whence the supply flowed, one morning called at his house, and with her eyes swimming in tears of gratitude, blessed and thanked him for his noble generosity, of which she was no longer in need, a reputable and opulent tradesman of Calcutta, who was perfectly well acquainted with her private history, having proposed marriage, and previously to settle thirty thousand sicca rupees upon her, an offer she had accepted, and therefore had no longer occasion to trespass upon his bounty, a grateful remembrance of which would remain indelibly fixed in her mind while life remained. Nothing distressed this excellent man more than his acts of benevolence becoming publicly known, for ostentation had nothing to do with his innumerable charities.

Lure of Money

Social life at the military stations revolved around dances, dinner parties and sport. It was customary for army officers to encourage contacts between their marriageable daughters and upcoming eligible bachelors. Many marriages were thus solemnized at these stations dubbed 'golden ghettos' of British rule. The more accomplished among the girls who had been educated in England, however, did not fancy army life, which they found boring and confined. They were not satisfied with being merely companions to their husbands in that totally male-oriented environment. The ambitious ones looked out for affluent suitors from other walks of life, even from countries other than their own.

H. Hervey in his well-known work The European in India *(1913) gives a bird's eye-view of the lifestyles of different classes of British people living in India. These include army officers, soldiers, civilians, other professionals and also young women, both married and unmarried. Here is a lively account of one young miss and her matrimonial adventure.*

In many a rakishly disposed man's life there comes a period when he sickens of aught that smacks of the hazardous so often conspicuous among our women in India, especially the married ones. It is when he contemplates matrimony that this nausea takes hold of him. However ardently he may have admired such sorceresses at one time, yet, when his mind is sobered, his heart implicated, he seriously considers the pros and cons of entering the Holy Estate, and he finds a legitimate object for his purer affections, when that which once proved so seductive becomes dust and ashes, bitter as Dead Sea fruit to his taste.

Thus was it with Redoak of the Cavalry. Till Miss Maud Lake appeared on the scene, that gallant sabreur had been a slave to the Fast Married Woman, specimens of whom are to be found in most Indian stations. But when Miss Lake joined her parents from home, he experienced the revulsion of feeling above referred to, and became desperately smitten. Colonel and Mrs Lake did not object to Redoak. True, they were cognizant of his penchant for other men's property, and had heard sundry items of *gup* that did not redound to the young fellow's credit; but when he grew so *epris* with their daughter, and entirely dropped Mrs This and Mrs That, they judged him to have turned over a new leaf, and that he meant honestly by the fair Maud. Moreover, knowing him to be of good family, though poor, and that he was otherwise steady, they were inclined to encourage him as a suitor for their daughter's hand—because one of the strongest Anglo-Indian [earlier the term Anglo-Indian was used for all British residents in India] tenets is 'to marry your girls off as fast as possible'. Miss Lake, however, was wiser in her generation. While entertaining a respect for 'blood', she fully understood the significance of limited means; for beyond a colonel's pay, her parents had nothing in the shape of income. Consequently, she would be a tocherless bride; so it behoved her to look out for a man with money, as she had been imported to India with the express purpose of getting 'settled in life'. Redoak, therefore, without being actually dismissed by the young lady, received very little countenance from her, and the only comfort the poor fellow derived was from the fact that Miss Lake favoured no one else; although the girl was attractive enough to vex the soul of an anchorite.

Affairs continued in this state for some months, and when the hot weather commenced, Miss Lake—like most newcomers—felt its effects so seriously that the old people packed her off to stay with some friends on the hills till the blessed monsoon broke, and made existence on the plains more bearable. When she returned, four months later, it was patent to all a great change had been wrought in her. Some surmised one thing, some another. From being affable, companionable, the girl scarcely acknowledged her former friends, and put on such an amount of 'side' that everyone wondered. At last, in about a week's time, the whisper went round that Miss Lake, while on the hills, had engaged herself to be married! Then the question arose, 'Whom to?' It was too delicate a query to put point-blank to the girl or her parents—the more so as all three preserved a strict silence on the subject. The fact of the engagement oozed out through the Lakes requesting the Chaplain to arrange for the ceremony on a certain day. His reverence naturally said something about it to his Eurasian church clerk, who, as naturally, gave out the news in the bazaar, and soon the whole station rang with the tidings. Then the date of the wedding was bruited: people inferred that the happy man would arrive a little before the marriage day, and everyone stood on the tiptoe of expectation, in the meanwhile figuratively moving heaven and earth to find out who the fellow was. Lady friends of Mrs Lake called informally on her, and insidiously endeavoured to worm out the secret; men buttonholed the

Colonel at the club, and sprung feelers on him in the shape of congratulations: but to no purpose—although the Lakes parried these advances with evident hesitation in their manner, that did not escape the notice of their inquisitors. The only one to tackle Miss Lake herself was Redoak, who, determining to probe the enigma, laid wait for her as she took her usual morning constitutional.

'Do tell me who he is!' he pleaded.

'I shall not satisfy your vulgar curiosity, Mr Redoak!' she replied angrily.

'I conclude he is in the Service?'

'Come to any conclusions you like.'

'Does he live on the hills, or is he a visitor?'

'I refuse to answer you.'

'Some old chap, I bet, and you do not care to own it, eh?'

'I shall not tell you.'

'Why are you not inviting guests to your wedding?'

'Is that any business of yours?'

'Suppose not, but it looks funny. What sort of a fellow is he in appearance?'

'I am not going to describe him for your edification or anyone else's. He'll be here on view in a few days, when you can all see for yourselves.'

'Do you think you'll be happy with him?'

'Do you think I would accept him did I fear otherwise?'

'He'll not make you so good a husband as I would, I'll take my oath.'

'You may take any oaths you please.'

'I would have devoted my all to you!'

'Your all!—consisting of a cavalry subaltern's pay; scarcely enough to keep you—much less a wife!'

'I shall rise in due course.'

'In due course—yes; but in the meanwhile? And-and if a family should come?'

'Well, that's only to be expected.'

'Perhaps so. But look around: who is well off here? Who is not more or less in debt? My father, for instance—colonel though he is, and drawing good salary, how much can he allow me for dress and things?'

'Humph! Your coming out of your shell a bit on the lucre part of the question makes me suspect that he's a rich fellow. Is he?'

'I shall not enlighten you.'

'Some foreigner, eh?—some globe-trotter you've caught on the hop. Isn't that it?'

'I decline to tell you.'

'Great Scott, you are close! At all events, will you say if he is a gentleman—worthy of you?'

'I shall not! Good morning!' And she turned in at her gate, leaving Redoak in as thick a fog as ever.

The following appeared in the *Weekly Hill Excelsior*, which arrived a day or so later on:

Another instance of transatlantic 'push' has been exemplified in our midst. The great Chicago millionaire pork-packer, Mr Ebenezer Mayflower, sojourning here in the course of a world's tour, has wooed and won—all within the space of a month—a young English lady well known at ——, who had been staying on these hills for the sake of her health. Mr Mayflower is reputed to be one of the richest men in the States.'

'A darned pig-killing pork butcher!' fumed Redoak, as he read the above at the club that evening.

'Yes; isn't it a beastly shame?' observed a man, overhearing him. 'Anyhow, she has kept her eye on the main chance and won't want for dollars. If they do send out invites for the wedding on Monday, will you go, Redoak?'

'Not I! I should want to convert the fellow into some of his own sausage meat! I've no wish to be hauled up for murder!'

The Grass Widow

Among the legacies of the Raj are the hill stations opened up by the British in the nineteenth century. These cool and pleasant spots provided an escape from the searing heat of the plains and a resort for the pleasure-seeker. It often happened that while the husband sweltered in the plains, the wife entertained herself with the company of civil and military men spending their leave in the hills. There was said to be a hotel in one of the hill stations where the manager would ring a bell in the mornings telling his guests to return to their own beds!

This story is taken from The European in India *(1913) by H. Hervey.*

The dictionary describes the term 'Grass Widow' as 'a wife temporarily separated from her husband', or 'one deserted by her husband', or 'a divorced woman'. The first interpretation will best suit the spirit of this story.

The Grass Widow is a prominent feature of Anglo-Indian life. Not that the genus is peculiar to that country alone, but she is more in evidence there. She—in common with her fellow-exotics—is one of the comparative few; so any idiosyncrasy on her part comes to the front without much effort.

191

There are Grass Widows and Grass Widows, some of the more captivating of whom gain for themselves a certain notoriety, not always desirable. They chiefly affect hill stations, whither they resort as soon as they are free of their husbands; though some remain on the plains during their lords' absence, not from choice, but probably because the house is their own, and they wish to save extra expenditure. Grass Widows are evolved from various causes, of which a war is the most fruitful. When the red (khaki) coats go to either of our frontiers, into the 'Buffer State', to China, or South Africa, the well-off ones ship their wives home; but those who cannot, send them to the hills, there to vegetate or amuse themselves till the husband's return—i.e., if he is not shot or otherwise disposed of. If plague, pestilence, or famine breaks out, it is the black coats' turn, and they are shunted in all directions over the stricken area. If the visitation threatens to be prolonged, the wives of the bloated Covenanted Civilians of course go home; but the Uncovenanted women, and others similarly lacking the means, either resort to the hills or remain where they are.

It is a strange and curious fact that you seldom, if ever, encounter an old, done-with-the-sweets-of-life woman who goes by the appellation of Grass Widow. As a rule, they are still on the sunny side of forty—a critical period in India for those of our fair ones who are not encased in a panoply of the soundest moral principles; because frequently a girl who was simply mediocre when twenty substantially improves with time, and at double that age becomes far more 'fetching' in her mellowness than she was in her callow days.

Mrs Amanda Orkney is the wife of an Uncovenanted man, who being put on special famine duty has to go under canvas miles in the district, and rough it there for perhaps six months. Mrs Orkney, who cannot stay on the plains by herself through the coming hot weather, goes to the hills. But she does not patronize the nearest, more fashionable range; she knows that several other ladies of the station are already there, or intend going. She does not much fancy their propinquity: they are jealous of her superior attraction; for their remarks—in which 'Madame Rachel', and 'all made up', and such-like pleasantries, are interlarded—have reached Mrs Orkney's ears; so she does not want to be under their surveillance while on her holiday. Therefore, when Orkney goes, she betakes herself to a little sanatorium far to the south, where she hopes to be free of such spite. Arrived at the solitary hotel, she cons the local directory, and a glow suffuses her cheek as she comes to one name. She engages a vacant furnished house, situated in a secluded spot, and that same evening moves over there with her servants and baggage. In the morning she is up betimes, and is taking her early tea when a horseman trots up to the portico, flings himself out of the saddle, and almost flings himself at the lady.

'So it is you Amanda! Thought I could not be mistaken when I saw your name last night in the list of arrivals at the club. But, heaven and earth!' he continues with a rush, holding her by the hands and running his eyes admiringly over her, 'how you have improved from the weedy girl I used to make love to coming out in the Poonah! Fifteen long years, wasn't it? I am glad we meet once more!'

'So am I, Mr Loughton,' she replies, colouring a little as she beams up at him. 'I-I-had an idea you were still on these hills, and was pleased to find your name in the directory yesterday.'

'Why were you pleased? We cannot spoon each other now.'

'N-no; but we can be friends, and I shall depend upon you to give me a good time up here. I know no one else.'

'I'll do my best,' he says, now dreamily and almost sadly; 'but, in spite of your sweet companionship, it will be uphill work for me, Amanda.'

'Hush! do not call me "Amanda". Remember I'm a married woman.'

'Yes, and must be treated as one, I suppose,' he remarks sardonically. 'What sort of a husband does Orkney make you?'

'A very good one; and I hope always to be a good wife to him.'

'Humph! Of course! Anyhow, I envy the fellow.'

'Hush again! Tell me, do you intend to remain a bachelor indefinitely?'

'I've not met my fate yet; but-but—'

'But what?'

'I should have—now, were you free!'

'Nonsense! We can like each other, nevertheless.'

'A difficult job for me—with the recollection of our voyage, now backed by meeting you again in all the glory of a splendid womanhood. And to think what I have missed! It's enough to send me daft.'

'Don't be silly! I recollect as well as you, and I find you just as nice now as you were then; yet I do not indulge in rhapsodies.'

'Ah, you are a woman; you handle the reins, hold the trump card in a game of this sort.'

'No sentimentalities!' she laughs. 'Finish your tea, and light up; perhaps a cigar will act as a sedative. Come, what is to be done up here?'

'Oh, the usual thing. You had better call round.'

'Are there any nice people?'

'A few; but mostly old folks—settled down on their properties. I see very little of the floating population, for I live two miles out.'

'On your estate?'

'Yes. I hope you'll come there and look me up. I shall feel like those fellows at Lystra, and think a goddess has visited me in the person of-er-your beautiful self!'

'More nonsense! What would Mrs Grundy say? I should require someone to play propriety.'

With sophistries such as these they continue the conversation for some time, till Loughton, carried away by his new-found infatuation, begins treading on dangerous ground, whereupon Amanda Orkney, still strong in her prudence, somewhat curtly dismisses him, with a hint not to repeat his visit. However, in a day or two she relents, and writes for him. He goes. He is humble; he realizes that she is not to be taken with a rush; so he shapes his behaviour accordingly. She relents more yet. she asks him to dine with her that night. He accepts the invitation. And the last thing seen of them is two figures seated side by side on a sofa in the dimly lighted veranda—the man's arm encircling the woman's waist, the woman's head reclining on the man's shoulder. But that, and no more!

A Woman of Pleasure

The oldest profession continued to thrive under the British. Lal bazars (red light districts) functioned in all Presidency towns and cantonments. Even white women, chiefly from East Europe, as well as Japanese girls were procured to staff the brothels in Calcutta and Bombay. Among the white women resident in India, those divorced by their husbands and unable to return home, ashamed of the disgrace they had brought on themselves, took to the flesh trade. The missionaries protested against this practice but the authorities felt that banning prostitution, which they felt fulfilled a socially necessary function, might lead to an increase in sexual offences.

This story of a woman driven into Mrs Warren's profession is drawn from H. Hervey's The European in India *(1913).*

'Make no deep scrutiny into her mutiny.'

Pity her, reader. Of all our country women in India, 'Perdita' calls for your passive—if not active—sympathy. She may owe her lapse to her own indiscretion; she may be the victim of man's lust; she may have bartered her virtue for gold: still, whatever the cause, there is always the other side of the question to consider; and if we go contrary to the spirit of the line above quoted, the probabilities are that most of these cases are attended with extenuating circumstances—in favour of the poor.

Without touching on the shoals of 'unfortunates' who, under 'The White Slave Traffic', are brought out chiefly from South-East Europe to the Presidency and a few, of the larger Indian cities, there are occasionally odd cases of British women to be found at the bigger up-country cantonments. She may be a lady by birth and education, who, having erred, and then figured in a divorce suit, is prevented by various reasons, from returning home; who, with her finer feelings dulled, and deserted by her undoer, casts all other considerations to the winds, makes for some garrison station far removed from the scene of her degradation, and regularly sets up as 'a woman of pleasure'. Again, she may be a girl of inferior social extraction, unmarried, seduced and abandoned by him whose specious assurances caused her to look for ultimate marriage; a scoundrel who turns a deaf ear to her when, on realizing his falseness, she implores him even to 'protect' her—for, being in a strange country, dishonoured and friendless, whom else can she seek succour from? This— in the early blush of her shame and perplexity; but in a short time, when she finds no other resources, and the first feeling of remorse wears off, she also goes down the broad path which, while leading to destruction, at all events tends to giving her a roof over her head and food for her sustenance, all wages of sin though she earns.

That little bungalow at the junction of Park and Artillery Roads had long been vacant because its last tenant, a European, died of cholera in it. When Mrs Vean—the 'Perdita'—first arrived, and as usual went to the travellers' bungalow, she inquired for small houses; and after viewing several, selected this one, caring nothing for the cholera story. The rent was low, the situation suitable, while the building itself stood retired from the road; so the next day she purchased furniture, engaged an indoor woman servant, and took possession. These preliminaries accomplished, it was time to break ground, as her store of money would require replenishing. She had privily ascertained from the travellers' bungalow female sweeper that there were no European 'ladies of easy virtue' in the place; the field was consequently open to her. So, after settling down, she proceeded to 'advertise' herself. She is a tall, fair, well-built woman of about thirty; and having brought her kit with her—by permission of a soft-hearted though outraged husband—she is able to attire herself attractively. The bandstand is not very far from her house; next Band evening, therefore, she strolled down to the rotunda in the park, and sat on one of the garden benches. Or course she created remark: ladies lolling in their carriages focused the handsome, well-dressed stranger; men glanced at her interestedly, wondering who she could be, and putting the question to each other.

Two officers in mufti drove up together in a dogcart, and slackened pace as they turned in to the circle surrounding the band-stand.

'Halloa!' muttered one, espying the solitary lady on, the garden seat; 'some newcomer. Who can she be?'

'Where?' inquired Captain Camden, the other, himself a comparatively recent addition to the place.

'There, by herself on the bench, with the figure, and that bottle-brush affair sticking up out of her hat.'

Camden looked, then suddenly pulled up, consigned the reins to his companion, and murmuring something about 'Think I've seen her somewhere', told his chum to drive on, that he would rejoin him later, alighted, walked across to the bench, and lifted his hat.

'Mrs Beathe, is it possible?' he exclaimed with pleased surprise, halting before her.

Mrs Beathe, alias Vean, glanced up nervously at him, coloured, looked round, and then rising, whispered, 'I am Mrs Vean here. I am glad to see you, Captain Camden; but this is too crowded for us to converse. Find a quiet spot somewhere, as I am new to the place, and—and—we may have, a deal to talk about.'

'Certainly, but why are you under another name?' he queried, in a tone of mystification.

'Hush! You will know presently.'

In a few minutes they had moved out of the crush; their going off in company being productive of much comment and remark.

'Let's see,' resumed Camden pleasantly, when quite out of earshot. 'The last time I had the pleasure of meeting you was over a year ago, at Rainuggur, while I attended the manoeuvres there; and the night before I left, you gave me several dances at the Cavalry Ball. By the way, where is Beathe? and how is he?'

'Have you not heard?' she murmured.

'Heard what?'

'That-that-he divorced me?'

'Divorced you?' ejaculated Camden, starting as if he had been shot. 'So that's why you have adopted a pseudonym! But it was not in the papers!'

'No: I believe Major Beathe took steps to prevent it appearing.'

'Good heavens! And-and-did you er-give—'

'Yes! I did give him cause. It is no use my beating about the bush. Do you remember Mr Haggerston?'

'Of the Survey—up there? and-and-with whom—now I think of it—you were rather chummy?'

'Yes. Well-er—' And she turned away her head, sobbing.

'I see, I see,' rejoined Camden reflectively, realizing the truth. 'And your husband?'

'He divorced me, as I have said. When the discovery was made, followed by the decree, Mr Haggerston, like the reptile he has proved himself, ran away home, and has returned my letters unopened, which shows the nature of the love he professed for me, and his pie-crust promises to marry me on getting the divorce. My husband, however, was very generous: he gave me some money above my steamer fare home, and allowed me to take my clothes and other personal property. His last words to me were, "Go in peace",' she concluded, with a sigh.

'Humph! And why have you not gone home?'

'Can you ask it? How could I—after what has happened—face my people?'

'Then what are you doing here?' queried Camden, becoming fogged again.

Diverging to a secluded bench, and motioning him to sit beside her, she told him all: her husband's attentions to another woman; her own sin—committed partly to revenge herself on him; the heads of the legal proceedings; her perplexities, her struggles, and her final decision to. become what she now was. 'In fact, I am "Perdita",' she faltered, with a lump in her throat and tears in her eyes. 'True, a life of dishonour is before me; but what alternative is there? I am branded, and even did I know some profession or calling which might earn me an honest livelihood, who would employ me?—for my story is sure to leak out sooner or later. I have no friends here. Some at Rainuggur, I dare say, would have been kind, but I was ashamed 'to remain there among them—ashamed to return home to my parents. Fate has thrown me across you in this place; you are my only acquaintance. Will you befriend me?'

'Too glad—if you will say how,' observed the unsuspecting Camden.

'Well,' she replied, her voice hardening, 'tell your men chums that—that—I am here.'

'As Mrs Beathe?'

'N-no; as-as—"Perdita".'

'*Haud ignara mali miseris succurere disco*,' said Camden to himself as he called to mind his own misfortunes, his own sins; and thinking that as this woman had verily and indeed burnt her boats behind her, the best way to answer her appeal was—to comply with her request. Poor thing!

From Affinity to Adultery

Love Potions, Amulets and Medicaments

There are amusing accounts of the use of talismans, amulets, charms and medicaments by some Indian women to win over their masters. For their latent virtues and mysterious powers these aids were said to be effective especially for tackling jealousy, revenge and other passions prevalent in the zenana. These were prescribed by wise women skilled in astrology and fortune-telling described by ancient poets as enchanters, diviners and charmers. James Forbes, a company officer who spent seventeen years in India, in his voluminous journal, Oriental Memoirs (1813) describes how these wise women were consulted by lovesick young people in India to captivate their objects of desire. As an illustration he presents an interesting episode of an Englishman and his Indian mistress.

The Moguls, Persians, Arabians, and most of the Asiatics, believe in genii, angels, and supernatural agents of various denominations, and degrees of existence; their histories, tales and romances, abound with such imagery. Some are the friends and guardians of the human race; others, called the evil genii, are in a constant state of warfare with the benevolent spirits. On this account, talismans, amulets, and charms, esteemed for their latent virtues, and mysterious powers, are worn by the inhabitants of India. They believe that such preparations are effective against witchcraft, fascination, and all the operations of the malevolent genii: they serve also as guards and protectors of hidden treasures, which are frequently buried under the earth, to conceal them from the avarice of the ruling despots.

The Greeks and Romans were not exempt from these prejudices, nor is it long since they have subsided in England. Acts of parliament on this subject, were passed so late as the reign of James the First. In the age of chivalry, enchantment and divination prevailed throughout Europe and in the oath administered by the constable to the combatants in a duel, are these expressions:

'Ye shall sweare that ye shall have no stone of virtue, nor hearbe of virtue; nor charm, nor experiment, nor none other enchantment by you; and that ye trust in none other thinge properly, but in God, and your body, and your brave quarrel.'

There are in most cities in India, a class of females, skilled in astrology, geomancy, and fortune-telling; these women were well known among the Greeks and Romans; and in our translations from the Hebrew they are called wise-women, which exactly answers to their appellation amongst the modern Indians. Wise ladies of this description are now consulted by young people in India, on the same subject; especially on the jealousy, revenge, and other passions prevalent in an Asiatic zenana. I could recite many modern anecdotes similar to those in Persian and Arabian tales, but will confine myself to that above alluded to.

A young English gentleman, when collector in one of the Company's districts in Guzerat, separated from all European society, formed a temporary connection with an amiable

Hindoo (sic) girl. For this step no justification is offered, though the most virtuous would, perhaps, make some allowance for influence of climate and custom, a total seclusion from European refinement and elegant society; and the impossibility, thus situated, of forming an honourable union with one of his fair countrywomen. In a Christian country, where every man, from the sovereign to the cottager, may wed the object of his affections, and where individual example influences the circle in which he moves, a deviation from moral rectitude admits not of this extenuation; but when seduction or adultery aggravate the crime, the evil strikes deep at moral and religious principle, and destroys domestic comfort.

The example of this young Englishman could have little effect among a people who neither professed the religion, nor practised the manners of Europe. His attachment to Zeida was constant, delicate, and sincere; he never saw her at her own house, and she entered his residence by a private door in the garden. Three years had passed in this manner, when one evening the lovely girl, her eyes suffused in tears, informed her protector that knowing he would shortly return to Europe, a cavalry officer of a good family in her own caste, had offered to marry her; a proposal she never would have listened to, had he remained in India; but under the idea of losing him, she requested his counsel on a scheme so important to her happiness. Her friend, delighted with this honourable establishment, readily consented, and the marriage took place. Zeida lived with her husband in a remote part of the city; from prudential reasons all former intercourse ceased; and from the different modes of life between Europeans and Asiatics, nothing was heard of Zeida for many months.

In the warm nights preceding the rainy season, the youth generally slept upon a sofa, placed under a gauze mosquito-curtain, on the flat roof of the house; to which there was one ascent from the interior, and another by an outer flight of steps from the garden. While reposing there on one of those delightful moon-light nights known only between the tropics, and apparently in a dream, he thought something gently pressed his heart, and caused a peculiar glow, accompanied by a spicy odour, which impregnated the atmosphere. Under this sensation he awoke, and beheld a female reclining over him in a graceful attitude. Her personal charms, costly jewels, and elegant attire were discernable through a transparent veil, a double fold artfully falling over the upper part concealed her features. Her left hand contained a box of perfumed ointment, with which her right was softly anointing his bosom, nearest the region of the heart. Doubtful whether the scene was real, or the effect of a warm imagination, he remained for some moments lost in astonishment; when the lovely stranger, throwing aside her veil, discovered Zeida, decked with every charm that youth and beauty could assume on such an interesting visit.

When his surprise subsided, Zeida informed him the marriage had turned out unfortunate. In the hope of happier days she had hitherto avoided troubling him with complaints; but seeing no improvement in her lot she seized the opportunity of her husband's absence to come to him with hopes of regaining that affection which had formerly constituted her happiness. Fearful of a cool reception, she had previously consulted the most celebrated cunning-woman in the city; who prepared a box of ointment, which she was to apply by stealth, as near as possible to the heart of the object beloved; and, if so far successful, she might be assured of accomplishing her wishes. Zeida knew not the character of her friend; he resisted the tear of beauty, and the eloquence of love; and having convinced her of the difference between their former attachment, and the crime of adultery, persuaded her to return home before the approaching dawn discovered the impropriety of her visit.

A Chronicle of Death Foretold

During the 18th and early 19th century before the advent of steam-shipping and opening of Suez Canal, sailing vessels used to take five to six months to cover the voyage from England to India. So the voyage to and fro kept the sailors away from home for nearly a year. In the absence of any communication facilities it was hard for the families to put up with such long separation especially for the old parents who prayed to have their sons near them while departing for the unknown. Such was the case of one sailor George Harcourt who lost his mother while on a voyage and also had a tragic end pining for his love. In the course of his voyage to India, Lt. Thomas Bacon was struck by the personality of George Harcourt, the ship's chief mate whose unobtrusive and gentlemanly deportment won him the esteem and goodwill of all on board. Bacon describes him as a fine, handsome fellow about thirty years of age who seemed to be suffering under some acute mental agony and disappointment. Bacon expressed his deep sympathy over his situation and after giving him consolation persuaded him to unburden his heart to him. In his journal, First Impressions and Studies from Nature in Hindostan *(1837) Bacon narrates in detail Harcourt's tale as told to him. A verbatim account in the first person is given below.*

I am certain in my heart that I shall never see the cliffs of my native land again, I am persuaded, by a vague unaccountable conviction, that some dreadful happening stands between me and my home. Home, did I say? The wide world is my only home now; but I know this is my last voyage upon the elements of this world. Before these planks and ropes are again in British water, my decaying body shall lie in the cold grave, or be thrown overboard as food for the fishes.

This is a terrible conviction, but though I struggled hard at first, I could not divest my mind of it, and now every passing day serves but to confirm the idea. You shake your head; now recollect my words: the day will speedily come when you will say, 'Ah! Poor fellow, he told me it would be so.' But it is not the death itself that I so dread, that I could contemplate with little agitation or regret; it is the probable consequence of my death when the tidings shall reach England, from this I flinch.

It is just about four years since I returned from a tedious and protracted voyage to China; and as soon as the duties of the ship permitted my absence from her, I hastened to the arms of an aged mother, who from the unusually protracted absence of our ship, and from accounts which had reached England of damages we had sustained in a hurricane off Bourbon, would I knew be more than ever anxious to embrace her only child. She had been a widow since the days of my boyhood, and subsisted frugally upon a small annuity, barely sufficient for her comfort, even when afterwards eked out by the poor pittance of my slender pay. She had, however, a pretty cottage upon the banks of the Thames near Richmond; and her love for her boy, her wish to supply him with every thing which could enhance his pleasure or his comforts, had induced her more than once to receive into her little household lodgers of known worth and respectability.

Oh! What a lovely glowing evening it was that saw me hastening from the stage-coach down to our little retreat. As I approached nearer, I remarked that the house had been enlarged and newly painted, and there were many little improvements and alterations about the garden, giving the place an air of greater comfort and importance than it had before possessed. I hastened to the door and knocked gently. Some moments elapsed before my summons was replied to, and I was just framing a word or two of greeting for honest Mary, my mother's only servant, when a footman, in a handsome but unassuming livery, stood before me. The blood fled back to my heart, and a cold perspiration burst out upon my forehead: in an instant I remembered that I had been more than twelve months from home. 'Where is my mother?' I demanded of the man. 'Mrs. Harcourt is upstairs, sir,' said he, respectfully inviting me to enter. 'I will let her know.' I was about to rush up before him, when he checked me by the arm—'Excuse me, sir, but you cannot see your mother just at this moment; she is asleep.' I dashed his hand aside, and springing up the narrow staircase, I entered my mother's room. All was silent as the grave, and the curtains were drawn; some labelled vials on the dressing table, and other unerring tokens, told me at once the truth. I hastened to the bed, and with breathless apprehension drew back the curtain. My mother lay sleeping, her left hand extended, and in the gentle grasp of one, who, even in the presence of my sick mother, engrossed my attention.

Oh! she was, indeed a beautiful girl. But I will not attempt to describe her, further than to mention, that she was exceedingly fair, with very light hair, but a deep lustrous blue eye, which gave token of a fervid soul. In figure, she was small and delicate in the extreme, and very graceful; so slight was her form, that it made one continually apprehensive lest anything evil should happen to her. She was sitting, or rather resting, upon the arm of a chair drawn close to the bed; her disengaged hand held some lace, upon which she had been working; and as she raised her fine eyes to mine, a faint exclamation of surprise escaped her. She put her finger on her lips. 'Hush! your mother sleeps. Thank God, you have returned.' She then rose, and gently disengaging her hand, left the room, beckoning me to follow her. She went into the little front drawing-room, and taking me by the hand, said, 'O, sir, your mother has been very ill for some months past, and your long absence has, I fear, affected her health. I am so very glad you have returned. She, dear woman, has been really somewhat better lately, and I trust we may look for some improvement. She speaks of nobody but you; and the last few days have been spent in incessant prayers for your return.'

After some further conversation relative to my dear mother, she said: 'But are you not surprised at my boldness? You do not even yet know who I am, and I have been talking to you thus familiarly. You must excuse me: we are well acquainted with your portrait, which hangs over the mantelpiece there, and with yourself too, from your dear mother's conversation. Half an hour's further conversation put me in possession of the following facts regarding this sweet girl and her father. They had been travelling on the Continent, and on their return to England, being taken with the homely beauties of my mother's cottage, while passing down the river, had come to lodge in the house some eight months previous to my return to England. Two or three months' intercourse, though only occasional, between the hostess and her lodgers, had given rise to a mutual regard; which gradually ripened into a warm affection, when, during my mother's very dangerous illness, this lovely girl spared no pains in taking care of her.

The tea-things had just been brought in when the old father of my beautiful young companion entered. The pretty girl hastened into the passage to meet him, and give him the news of my arrival. He came in, and welcomed me home with utmost warmth and affection.

The next morning found my mother considerably better and stronger than she had been for many weeks; and you may conceive the delight that my reappearance gave her and she was again active and moved about the house almost as well as ever. In the meantime as my ship was under extensive repairs, I had leisure to take watch-and-watch-about with my beautiful friend. Sometimes—nay, nearly always—we watched together, read together, sang together, and walked together. In fact, we were seldom separate, except when business required my presence at the dock. Excuse these tears: I fondly recall those hours of pure delight. while dependant upon each other for amusement and pastime. The old gentleman treated me as if I had been an only son; and, indeed, the most implicit confidence existed among us all: and never once, during my four months' stay at home, did an unpleasant incident arise to damp, even for a moment, the pleasure of our intimacy.

How few, how transient, are such hours as these! If we look for a continuance of such in this life, we shall assuredly be disappointed. The day came for my departure, and it was not till then that I felt, with its full weight, the new attachment to that sweet home. I bade my dear mother a fond adieu; and Ellen, with an unbidden tear standing in her eye, gave me her hand; I kissed it with a swelling heart, and hastened away.

Twice or thrice did I thus return to my dear home, and still found it the same, without a change. The Grahams had become a part of our family; and, although no vows of affection had passed between Ellen and me, yet it appeared to be tacitly understood by all that something more than the attachment of cold regard existed between us; and before I left home, in 1829, my mother gave me to understand that it was the mutual wish of Mr Graham and herself to see my Ellen and me ultimately united, for better for worse.

We made a prosperous and speedy passage to India, and when homeward-bound, touched at the Cape of Good Hope, to land passengers and take in stock. I had strolled with a friend to the public library and reading-room, and by mere chance, in running my eye over the columns of an English newspaper I came suddenly upon the notice of my mother's death; too circumstantial, alas! to leave hope of a mistake. At last we arrived in town, and without a moment's delay I hurried down to Richmond, where my worst fears were of course confirmed. My house I found in the hand of strangers, and now indeed I felt myself an outcast upon the face of the wide world. There was not even a trace of my own Ellen, and the vulgar footman in yellow livery, who answered my summons to the door, replied to my inquiries. 'How the devil should I know?'

I returned to the ship depressed and spirit-broken, and as I stepped on board, a porter put a note into my hand. I scarcely heeded him, believing it to be some business connected with the ship, but by habit I glanced at the address. Good God! how my heart leaped with gratitude and delight: it was my Ellen's handwriting. I read as follows:

I have just heard of the arrival of your ship; God grant that you may have returned in health and safety: but, alas! ere this you must have heard all; your dear mother's affairs were placed by my beloved father in the hands of Messrs. P. and Co. of No. 3,—— street, just before his death: you will there find her last letters and bequests to you. My dear father had, at your mother's solicitation, undertaken to perform the offices of her executor and your guardian, and he pledged himself ever to think of you, and to treat you as his own son, but he was not spared to fulfil even the former of these kindly parts, being suddenly snatched from us by a paralytic stroke, bequeathing me to the protection and guardianship of my mother's brother, a rich merchant in the above firm, whom you have more than once seen at Richmond. I cannot write more: you will find me at No.—, ——street.

Under all changes, believe me, ever the same,

ELLEN.

P.S. I do not say come speedily.

The next morning I called, as Ellen had directed me, and saw how changed was she, beautiful indeed, perhaps more so than ever, but pale and delicate in the extreme. The slight blush her cheek wore on my first entrance rapidly faded, and I saw it no more. 'Have you not seen my uncle?' she inquired; 'he left the house to seek you.' I told her I had not seen him; and I observed her loverly bosom heaving with more than common emotion. She burst into a fearful fllood of tears, and presently, while I still endeavoured to soothe her, exclaimed, 'Oh! George, I have much to tell you. If you really feel, as I believe you do, you have another severe trial to go through. Tell me, have you heard nothing about me since we parted?'

I gasped for breath; I fancied I saw it all. 'What is it, my Ellen? tell me, or you will drive me mad.'

With many tears and sobs of bitter anguish she explained as follows. 'At the time of my father's death, my uncle was out of town, and did not receive his summons to the last scene till all was over. Among his last papers, my father wrote a letter to my uncle, detailing to him the views and intentions of our mutual parents regarding our union, and requesting that if no impediment should intervene, our nuptials might take place on my becoming of age. In his will he bequeathed to me his entire property (with the exception of a few small legacies), amounting to 22,000 Pounds; but, oh! George, how can I tell it you? my uncle vows I never shall be yours, and is trying to force me into an alliance with his utterly detestable son. The tyranny I have suffered under this roof has been almost too much for me to bear; indeed my heart must break.' I did all I possibly could to reassure and calm her, asserting the impotence of her uncle's threats to dispose of her hand contrary to her own wishes. I was about to take my leave when Mr.Pitman entered the hall. Ellen trembling introduced us, for she had followed me to the door.

'Oh, ho! young man, you're here, are you? A vastly pretty trudge I've had down to the docks and back after you, and now I find you here.' I told him politely, that I had come to pay my respects to him and his niece; that I presumed he was aware of the strong friendship which had existed between myself and Miss Graham's father, and the peculiar understanding, amounting almost to a pledge, under which I had quitted England. 'And pray, sir,' said he, 'how did you know, or what business had you to find out that my niece, Miss Graham, was living in my house, and under my protection, sir? ' With a supercilious display of mock courtesy, he now begged the honour of my company in his study, whither I followed him. He closed the door with a bang as vast as himself, and throwing himself into a large easy chair, motioned me to a music stool. I quietly put it on one side and seated myself in a chair. He eyed me for some time in profound silence, with an expression of bullying insolence. I broke the pause.

'May I beg, sir, to be favoured with the object of this private interview, for such I presume it is intended to be.'

I should wish to be useful to you, young sir, as you were a friend of my late brother-in-law; that is, if I find you deserving of my patronage. The command of a clipper is, I suppose, the very summit of your ambition; is it not?'

'Sir, you are particularly obliging, but I request you will consider me sincere and decisive in at once declining your offer of patronage. I cannot feel that I have any claims on your generosity except in regard to your niece, who was——'

'My niece, sir! What the devil have you to do with my niece, sir?'

'Her father, sir—'

'Her father, sir! What the devil have you to do with her father, sir? When her father was alive, she was her father's daughter, and now he's dead, she's my niece, sir; just as much mine, sir, as any other piece of household stuff bequeathed to me.'

'Very true, sir; but we have been for the past twelve months as—'

'You have been, sir! Yes, you have been for the past twelve months a couple of fools, laying plans for the future, without considering that the odds are ten to one they would never be fulfilled. My niece is my niece, and neither dead men nor live men shall interfere with my plans for her future life; she shall marry just as I think fit to give her away, without reference to the dead, or you, or herself either. Now, sir, how do you like that?'

'I protest sir, against—'

'You protest, sir! who the devil are you, sir? You protest, indeed! vastly good! You, a wandering vagabond, with a penniless purse and a ragged shirt! Upon my honour, vastly good! vastly good, indeed!!! But, hark ye, sir; I may be induced to forgive you this insolence, if you promise to behave well in future—take my advice, think of it; and I may help you to make your fortune yet, if you are wise.'

I had risen from my seat in indignant rage, maddened by his insulting language. My blood boiled almost to suffocation, and but for the sake of my Ellen, I should have floored him there and then.

Ellen had retained her old servant, John, and through him we succeeded in carrying on a correspondence for some weeks. She told me of much harsh treatment which she experienced from her uncle, and did not conceal from me that her health was sinking daily, but rather spoke happily in anticipation of an early release from her misery. Twice or thrice we met for a few minutes by appointment, but I had much difficulty in prevailing upon her to indulge me in this; and each time I saw her I noticed her growing paler and weaker by the day.

She one day fixed an appointment to meet me in the park, but in her place came John. Tears glistened in his eyes as he said, 'Ah, sir, my sweet young mistress is taken very ill; I'm afraid she's not long for this world; poor dear young lady, she was never used to hard words, and can't bear it.'

John also told me that he feared personal violence had been inflicted on her; for upon one occasion he had fancied that he heard his young mistress crying in piteous accents for mercy, and entering the room under some pretext, he found Mr.Pitman almost frenzied with the violence of his anger, and poor Ellen lying almost senseless upon the couch. Afterwards it was seen that poor Ellen's face was sadly bruised, but this the brutal man affirmed had been done by a fall during a fit of hysterical excitement.

From this time John brought me daily accounts of her health, and although until the time of my departure from England no immediate danger was anticipated, yet she continued too much an invalid to leave her couch, so that I was unable to bid her adieu, except by letter, and this I am convinced was my last communication with her in this world—the last of my Ellen; for I feel confident I shall not live to see England again; and my poor Ellen too, I fear, cannot last long under such treatment; remember what she had been used to.

Harcourt here concluded his touching tale, and Lt. Bacon endeavoured to reason him out of his despondency, telling him it was unmanly to give way to it, and that he should expect ere long to see him in command of a clipper, and master of his own little Ellen; but he could not shake his fatal presentiment. He shook his head, exclaiming, 'Mark my words, it will be as I say.'

Harcourt continued in the same melancholy state of mind until ship's arrival at Calcutta on the 3rd of August, 1831. A violent cold, which he had neglected, had settled on his lungs and became chronic. On that very day he was standing upon the starboard side of the quarter-deck giving directions about the cable, when a heavy rope, cast off from the main-top, struck him on the head and laid him senseless on the deck. He was immediately carried to his cabin, and was soon restored to consciousness; but the surgeon shook his head, and with good reason, for poor Harcourt never again recovered the use of his limbs. He was removed ashore to the house of a friend in Calcutta, where Bacon frequently visited him; it was evident that he was sinking fast into the grave; of this he was well aware, and often alluded cheerfully to his approaching end. On the 15th of August, twelve days after their arrival in Calcutta, Bacon followed with sincere mourning his remains to the burial ground at Chowringhee.

He concludes: This was the end of the excellent Harcourt—he told me it would be so. What has become of his Ellen? Has she taken the wings of a dove and flown to meet her devoted George? or has she become the humdrum wife of a counting-house clerk?

Sources

1. William Hickey and His Bibi Jemdanee: *Memoirs of William Hickey*, ed. Alfred Spencer, 4 vols. (London, 1913-1925)

2. Reminiscences of a Half-Caste: *The East India Sketch-Book*, by a 'Lady', Vol. I (London, 1833)

3. Revenge of the Native Mistress: *The East India Sketch-Book*, Anonymous, Vol. I (London, 1832). The original title of the story is 'Le vrai N'est Pas Toujours Le Vraisemblable'.

4. Begum Sumroo's Escapade: *Rambles and Recollections of an Indian Official* by Lt. Col W.H. Freeman (London, 1844)

5. The Intrigues of a Nabob: *Echoes from old Calcutta* by H.E. Busteed, 4th Edition (London, 1908)

6. Reunion at Nagpore: *The Manners and Customs of Society in India* by Mrs Major Clemons (London, 1841). The original title of the story is 'The Soldier'.

7. An Invisible Attraction: *Memoirs of a Griffin* by Capt. Bellew, 2 Vols (London, 1843)

8. Reminiscences of Shaik Ismael: *The East India Sketch-Book*, by a 'Lady', Vol II (London, 1833)

9. The Captain's Betrayal: *The Manners and Customs of Society in India*, by Mrs Major Clemons (London, 1841). The original title of the story is 'A Love Story'.

10. The Tank Tragedy: *Lays of Ind* by Aliph Cheem, 5th edition (Calcutta, 1883).

11. The Deserted Husband and the Criminal Lover: *The East India*

Sketch-Book, Anonymous, Vol I (London, 1832). The original title of the story is 'Management'.

12. Madame Grand's Great Passion: *British Social Life in India, 1608-1937* by Dennis Kincaid (London, 1938).

13. Marriage, A Take-in on Both Sides: *First Impressions and Studies from Nature in Hindostan* by Lt Thomas Bacon, Vol I (London, 1837)

14. The Faithless Fiancé: *The Manners and Customs of Society in India* by Mrs Major Clemons (London, 1841). The original title of the story is 'The Inconstant'.

15. The Hollow Tooth: *Lays of Ind* by Aliph Cheem, 5th edition (Calcutta, 1883)

16. Infatuation in Middle Age: *British Social Life in India, 1608-1937* by Dennis Kincaid (London, 1938)

17. A Marriage Made in Heaven: *First Impressions and Studies from Nature in Hindostan* by Lt Thomas Bacon, Vol I (London, 1837)

18. The Compassionate Judge: *Memoirs of William Hickey*, ed. by Alfred Spencer, Vol III (London, 1923)

19. Lure of Money: *The European in India* by H. Hervey (London, 1913). The original title of the story is 'The Attached Miss'.

20. The Grass Widow—Do

21. A Woman of Pleasure—Do. The original title of the story is 'Perdita'.

22. From Affinity to Adultery: *Orient Memoirs* Volume 4 by James Forbes, 1813.

23. A Chronicle of Death Foretold: *First Impressions and Studies from Nature in Hindostan* by Lt Thomas Bacon, Vol I (London, 1837)